MW00942153

First published in Great Britain in 2023

Copyright © Louiseee with three e's, 2023
Illustrations copyright © by Rob Page, 2023

www.louiseeewiththreees.com
www.robpageillustration.com

ISBN 978-1-7393722-0-0

ISBN 978-1-7393722-0-0

9 781739 372200 >

sign your name
in the box below...

...is a G.O.A.T
Greatest Of All Time

Louiseee with three e's - the author

Louiseee with three e's has been writing short stories which mirror her view on reality for many years. This is her first novel.

Her message to the world is to approach life as a goat would; be friends with everyone and don't worry about the rain.

Meet The Author:
www.louiseeewiththreees.com

Rob Page – the illustrator

Rob has been illustrating children's books for many, many years. When he is not illustrating he loves to travel the world, read books, watch movies and play computer games.

He loves history, mythical creatures and hunting for hidden treasures.

Meet The Illustrator:
www.robpageillustration.com

Meet some of the characters.

AMY

ÕOGLEY

SEBASTIÀN

MUM

COLIN

NORMAN

MS
TRUDY-WUDY

MRS
MOOPLETON

AMY THE
G.O.A.T

GREATEST OF ALL TIME

BY
LOUISEEE
WITH THREE E'S

ILLUSTRATED BY ROB PAGE

Happiness can exist only
in acceptance...as a goat.

- George Orwell -
(maybe)

Contents

1
Un-happy birthday!

"I can only apologise for the quick dinner," said Mum, plonking down a plate of bread and toast. "I'm in a bit of a rush tonight. It's the first dress rehearsal at circus training. We've got our big show opening in just a few weeks!"

Neither Amy nor Colin, Mum's new boyfriend, stopped eating to notice her flitting around. She pushed another crust of bread into the toaster.

"In just a few weeks I need to perfect the art of balancing on my head while riding on the back of a camel. It's not as easy as it sounds."

Colin took a large slice of toast. "Amy, could I trouble you for some marmalade?"

Amy pushed away from the table, balancing on the scrawny chair's back legs. She pulled open the dusty cupboard behind her.

"Ewww, its use-by-date is 1972," she said, inspecting a sticky, orange jar.

Eating stale, forgotten food that lurked in cupboards was quite normal in Amy's house. After Colin moved in following her parents' divorce, Amy learnt he was useless at a weekly food shop and Mum was too busy spending every second doing her activities. Be it tap dancing, yoga or circus skills, every evening she'd prance around the kitchen in her own world. "Everyone should always be striving for the best, not sat in front of the TV," she said daily… even when the TV was off…and no one was in.

Colin swallowed his mouthful. "1972 was an excellent year for marmalade."

"But it's got furry green bits in it."

"Oh, will you stop *moaning*, Amy," said Mum, pushing up to a headstand in the centre of the kitchen. Her bottom was right in Amy's eyeline.

"You're always trying to be different to everyone else, why don't you eat the mould."

Amy glared up at her Mother but was met by two firm bum cheeks in a blue leotard.

"Nonsense!" said Colin, taking the sticky jar. "We can both eat around it."

He rattled the tip of his knife, trying to find a less mouldy bit.

"Ahh, here we are," he said, smearing an orange clump on Amy's plate.

"Gosh, what a gift that is," she replied sarcastically, inspecting the bogey-looking lump.

Suddenly Colin's heavy thick eyebrows jumped up towards his hairline.

"Gift! That reminds me!" He dashed out of the kitchen, stumbling over himself as he pulled up his trousers that were forever falling down. Moments later he returned, biting his lips, fighting a big smile. He was holding a present beautifully wrapped with a green bow. "Happy birthday, Amy." He bent down and kissed her head.

This instantly made Amy smile. What a terrible day she'd had at her new school, St Andrews School of Controlled Excellence & Unoriginality. It's against the rules to celebrate birthdays and engraved on the school's large, iron gates is the motto:

CLOSE YOUR MIND
AND DO AS YOU'RE TOLD

At her school it was very important to Mrs Moopleton, the headmistress, that all pupils remained the same and didn't stand out. If they did stand out, she'd paint them. In thick, grey paint.

Some at Ofsted did question this, but she believed in a more hands on approach when dealing with naughty children. You can't simply *speak* to

them when telling them off, you have to cover and smother their soul!

However, Amy being Amy, had challenged this and worn a flashing birthday badge she'd made herself. In the morning assembly, Mrs Moopleton spotted it instantly.

"Stop thinking you're different to everyone else!"

She hissed in Amy's face, ripping the badge from her blouse, reaching for her paint brush.

Quickly, Amy tore through the wrapping paper to shut out the sadness. In her lap sat a bashed-up box smelling a bit like lemons. She carefully folded back the lid to see a collection of household cleaning products. There was a packet of yellow dusters, some carpet cleaner and a super-saver size bottle of lemon Fairy Liquid.

Colin grinned at his stepdaughter, trying to suppress his excitement. "You seem so interested when I'm cleaning so I thought it'd be nice to do some together." There was a twinkle in his eye.

To any other child, this may seem odd, but not to Amy. Colin tried very hard to build a relationship with his stepdaughter. He understood it couldn't have been easy for her to watch her parents separate and have her dad move out, and then have him, the new boyfriend, move in. So, he reached out the way he knew best: cleaning. He was allergic to almost

4

every single thing in the world (dust, animals...even fish and snails) so he was always vacuuming to keep off his sneezes. Quickly Amy learnt it wasn't normal to vacuum family members as they slept. Nor was it polite to spray disinfectant into the face of everyone who stepped into their house.

"Welcome to our home!" he'd shout, then spray and dash away.

Amy smiled down at the dusters and carpet cleaner, touched at Colin's gift.

"Thanks, Colin. That's really...um," she paused, finding the right words "...hygienic of you."

"Oh goodness!" shouted Mum, jumping down from her headstand. "Of course, it's your birthday *today*! The big nine...no, 10! I um...must have left your present in the car. Yes, that's right, it's in the car".

"I'll go get it shall I?" offered Colin, a mouth full of toast.

"No!" snapped Mum, eyes searching for the car keys. "It'll ruin the surprise! I'll go and get it. What was it you asked for again?"

Unlike most 10 year old's, Amy hadn't asked for anything. She knew what she wanted couldn't be bought with money. What she wanted was quite simply to be allowed to be herself.

You see, Amy felt people lived *painfully* dull lives. And for a 10 year-old girl, she was naturally quite... different. She thought differently, she felt differently and she smelt differently (we'll get to that later).

"Why don't people do what they *actually* want to do?" She'd mull over while doing something very different like wearing a dirty saucepan on her head, and walking around the house backwards.

"Why does everyone at school do the classes they don't want to do but told they *have* to. And then go to work...forever?"

"I've got it!" shouted Mum, interrupting Amy's train of thought. "Your present can be to come to my circus rehearsal tonight. It's our first dress rehearsal so you'll be the lucky girl who sees it before all your new friends. That's sure to impress the "*cool*" group at your expensive school -."

" - That's alright Mum!" interrupted Amy, her voice panicked and high-pitched. "I've got – um - a lot of...a lot of homework to do." She slid from her chair, ready to make a run for it.

Mum disco danced her way to the kitchen door, blocking the only exit. "Nonsense, it's your *birthday*. You don't have to do your homework." She paused, regretting such a silly suggestion. "Well, you can get up extra early and do it tomorrow morning before school."

"That'll be a treat!" piped in Colin.

"And you can come too."

Colin gulped loudly, swallowing his final crust.

Amy giggled at her stepdad. Recently the two of them had been dragged to a lot of Mum's shows. It involved them sitting around bored for hours.

All at once, the front door slammed and in strutted Sebastián. He dumped his rucksack on the floor, narrowly missing Stewart the cat, then dumped himself on a big bean bag slumped in the corner of the kitchen.

Now, one unimportant person we failed to

introduce earlier was Amy's big brother by four years, Sebastián. He wasn't like a normal big brother who would punch, pinch and fart. Instead, he did the meanest thing a big brother could do.

He completely ignored her.

He chose to believe Amy didn't exist.

"I can smell something," he announced, pointing the remote at the TV.

"Oh, that'll be the toast burning!" cried Colin, scurrying to the smoking toaster.

"No, I can smell something like, *really* disgustingly bad."

Amy glared at the back of her brother's head. He was talking about her. "Why don't you say what you think the smell is?" she shouted across the kitchen.

Sebastián acted out a big, drawn-out, yawn. His eyes never leaving the screen. This is what Sebastián did. He communicated with Amy by saying there was a bad smell. He found her repulsive so never spoke or looked at her. She was invisible to him. Most younger sisters would love to be ignored by their older brothers, just to have a break from the bullying. But not Amy. She longed to be tripped up or spat at. Anything that meant he saw her.

He even ignored her at their new school. What made it worse was he was already the most popular person there. He never said or did anything different but the children would flock and wait for him at the school gates for hours. To be fair, he was rather handsome for a 14-year-old. He'd had braces at a young age so his teeth were now perfectly straight. His hair was confusingly shiny and unlike most teenagers, he had only a thin covering of pimples

7

across his face. He took no interest in his classmates. His one focus was the cheerleading team. He had to become captain and this was his sole purpose for being alive. Having a smelly younger sister who tried to be different didn't help.

"Hello my dear, Sebastián!" sang Mum. "How was school? Did you learn anything that will change the world?"

Sebastián ignored her. He was still angry about Colin moving in so soon after Dad left. Not that Dad was ever around much before that anyway. He flicked through the music channels. Behaviour only *he* could get away with.

"That's excellent," replied Mum to the unanswered question. "And shall you be joining me at my circus rehearsal tonight? I'm not sure if I've mentioned, but it's the first dress rehearsal –"

"We know!" shouted Colin wafting the smoking toaster with a cloth.

"It's the first dress rehearsal for the Circus Society before our big day," she continued like she hadn't been interrupted, "and the whole family have decided to show their support."

"I thought it was for my birthday?" questioned Amy.

"Yes, and that too…I suppose," Mum squeezed Sebastián's left shoulder. "What do you say, My Little Hero?"

Sebastián wrinkled his nose at the words, 'My

8

Little Hero'. Mum called him this when she wanted him to do something for her.

"No. TV."

"Okay, that's fine. I'll leave out a big bowl of crisps and unlimited chocolate for you."

"That's not fair!" argued Amy. "It's *my* birthday."

Mum clapped her hands together showing the matter to be closed. "Right, now where did I hide the expensive chocolate?"

"But I don't want to go either, Mum!" said Amy, waving her hands, desperate to be seen.

"Nonsense, Amy. Now go change into something dull that doesn't reflect your personality. I don't want you attracting attention away from the clowns like last time."

Amy frowned deeply, glaring at the back of Mum's head. "I'm wearing my flashing birthday badge."

Mum flung round, throwing her arms in the air. "Absolutely not! These are important members of the circus we are trying to impress. I can't have you turning up, being 'different'."

"But -"

"Be gone!"

Mum shooed the girl away like a stray cat. Amy trudged up the stairs to her room, untying the fun rainbow ribbon from her bun.

"Ahh, I can finally smell fresh air," announced Sebastián loudly to make sure Amy heard.

Amy opened her mouth to shout something back but quickly felt there was no point. Would she ever be allowed to be her true self?

She was about to find out...

2
The circus

Amy and Colin sat on the rickety benches waiting for the show to begin. The tent was huge, filled with the smell of warm popcorn and donkey poo. The performers frantically rushed past them. One had a rubber chicken lodged under her arm, while another woman wore a heavy wig of purple afro hair that kept sliding off.

"All seems a bit chaotic," said Colin, shovelling salty popcorn into his mouth.

Amy shrugged. She was sulking and much to her annoyance Colin was too excited to notice. She wanted the next few hours to go by as quickly as possible.

All at once the lights dimmed and the audience hushed. The show was about to begin.

"Here we go!" squealed Colin, waving his flashing plastic sword (he originally bought this for Amy).

A very merry ringmaster bounced into the centre of the ring. His sweaty forehead sparkled more than his blue sequined blazer.

"Lords and ladies, are you ready to be entertained!?"

His eyes searched the silent audience of seven people. All of whom were unlucky family members that had been dragged along.

"I said…ARE YOU READY TO BE ENTERTAINED?"

"YeahhhHHHhhhh!" cheered Colin. Alone.

"This is our first dress rehearsal. Soon we will open our tent doors to the world!" he paused, waiting for applause that never came. "Tonight's show we have real animals and even a bit of riskeeeey dancing!"

Amy felt her body cringe at the thought of Mum wearing something short and sparkly while shaking her bottom a lot.

"Let's bring out our first act. It's Hulaaaa Hooooop Helennnn!"

The lights flashed so bright they stung the back of Amy's eyes. As she raised her hand to shield herself, she froze. Shocked at who was on stage.

"That's Mrs Dribblebum, my old maths teacher!" she shouted, jumping up from the bench. "She's almost 100! She retired *years* ago."

Mrs Dribblebum skipped to the centre of the stage like a bouncing antelope. She clearly had a lot of life left in her. Her body had lots of sharp edges with wrinkles of skin hanging from them. She proudly wore a fluffy pink bra and mini skirt.

"Evenin'," she said with a flirty wink in Colin's direction.

She stepped into a large striped hula hoop, lifted it to her waist then nodded at the young lad slouched on the DJ desk. Loud music started, and Mrs Dribblebum sent the hula hoop flying around her hips. Carefully she rocked back and forth to keep the hoop spinning in the air.

"Very impressive," whispered Colin.

Amy stared at the woman. "Is that it?"

She was hoping for something else to happen, but it didn't. Instead, Mrs Dribblebum held her chin high and simply smiled out to the audience, thrusting her hips back and forth...back and forth... for 40 long minutes.

"Very, *very* impressive," said Colin, 41 minutes later.

"Hmmm," yawned Amy, checking the empty box of popcorn. She sunk back on the bench, bored. "Can we go yet?"

The following acts were very similar. Soon Amy realised the circus was an odd jumble of people from town doing everyday things. Mr Bucket, the postman, came out and took Betsy, his black labradoodle for a walk around the ring. Then Mrs Hamedi from the bakery appeared and balanced on one leg (that was it!) Amy's own mother, as feared, wore tight red shorts and shook her bottom a lot.

By the final act, Amy had to blow into her hands to keep warm. For three hours she'd been sat in a cold tent, and on her birthday.

"Let's get on with it!" she shouted without looking up, not realising her own mother was still on stage. And then it happened.

Out marched the final act: Norman, the local milkman. Norman was a short, square man with chest hair so curly it looked like a hyper child had scribbled it on. On his head he wore the most marvellous top hat which had a long curly feather pointing out.

The milkman held his arms above his head and slowly belly danced. His stomach rippled up and then down to the beat of the music.

"Oh, here we go again," said Amy, rolling her eyes like a stroppy teenager. "This is the best one yet!" said Colin, grabbing Amy's folded arms and waving them above her head for her.

After a few minutes of this high-class entertainment, Norman led a farmyard goat out from the back curtain. The goat was beautiful. It was large for its breed with its back reaching up above the man's shirtless belly. It was completely black except for a peculiar white line of fur that started from its hoof, went up its knobbly leg and over its back to finish on a floppy ears tip. It was as if someone had held a heavy wet paintbrush and dribbled white paint over the animal. The goat looked out at the crowd, met Amy's eye and gave a smile.

Amy felt her stomach flip. She pulled at Colin's coat sleeve. "Look at that!"

"Oh I wish your mother had warned me, goats make me sneeze terribly...ACHOOO!"

"Shh, Colin! You're disturbing the show."

Norman the milkman skipped to the side of the ring and called, "tip tip tip tip." The goat was meant to follow him and crawl through a tunnel then jump over a big ball. But the goat didn't move. Somehow Amy knew it wanted nothing to do with the sweaty man. Instead, it trotted behind him, pushed up onto its back legs and with its big, square teeth, plucked the top hat from the man's head and put it on its own.

"Outsmarted by a goat!" giggled Amy as she watched the animal roll around on its back while wearing the man's hat. Amy couldn't help but think it looked better on the goat.

This made the milkman look very foolish and as a result, he was starting to get angry. He wiped the sweat from his forehead and marched to the side of the ring to a large wooden trunk. He clicked it open, leant in and took out a metal neck chain where a very shiny, very expensive looking whistle was hanging from it.

"I'm afraid you're not behaving very well, Mr Goat!" he said.

At once he blew hard into the whistle.

Weeeeeeeeeeeeeeeeet!!!!

The sound was deafening.

"Ahh, my ears!" screamed Amy, jumping to cover her stinging ears from the high pitched note.

He blew it harder, making the sound ring around the tent.

"It's not too bad for me!" shouted Colin down at Amy, pointing at his ears. "Something to look forward to when you're my age!"

"What!?" shouted Amy in response. Her hands were still protecting her ears so she couldn't hear a thing Colin had said. "That poor goat! It must be extra loud for her with her big ears!"

"What!?" shouted Colin back again.

Even with the whistle ringing out every second, the goat didn't do the tricks. Instead it was happily ignoring Norman, busy munching on some tangled wires. This made the angry milkman really stroppy. He stomped his feet and kept crossing then uncrossing his arms like a child about to have a tantrum.

"I've had enough of this."

He stomped across the circus ring and gripped the whistle so tightly his knuckles turned white. Sneaking up behind the goat, he bent down so that the whistle was right next to its large ears. The goat didn't suspect a thing. Then, he silently licked his plump lips, making sure they were nice and moist, and raised the deafening whistle up to them. He took a long, deep breath in, his hair chest expanding in size like a bouncy castle being pumped with air.

"No!" screamed Amy, grabbing Colin's large hands to shield her ears and eyes.

Then, as he went to blow, the cheeky goat spun round and ate his whistle in one. The whistle was never blown. Instead, the goat belched VERY loudly back into Norman's face.

Everyone froze.

"Hooray!" cheered Amy, breaking the silence. She leapt up, clapping so hard she felt her arms would fall off.

"Wait, what's happened!?" said Norman, as he started to rub the goats stomach trying to feel his whistle inside it.

At once, the show was over.

"Oh my," wheezed Colin. "Did you know I'm more allergic to goats than anything in the world." He patted down his trouser pockets, searching for a hanky.

Amy didn't hear him. She couldn't stop watching the defiant goat, who was now chasing Norman around the ring like a cartoon.

"They'll need to catch it ready for the next show," continued Colin, stretching his stiff back as he stood.

"I don't want them to catch it," moaned Amy. "It's not fair it has to do what Norman says."

"Oh, well it's not up to the goat I'm afraid… *achooo*."

"But it should be."

Suddenly the goat grew bored of chasing Norman and trotted to the side of the ring. It could easily jump out and escape, leaving the circus forever. In fact, the animal was thinking exactly this.

"Don't even think about it!" said Norman, squaring up to the creature. "You will be in big trouble, you hear me!"

"*Mehhhhh*," bleated the goat back at the man, still wearing his hat.

And just like that, the farm animal hopped over the ringside and trotted out of the tent. But before it was out of sight, it turned and met Amy's eye again.

"Look at it go!" said Amy feeling her stomach jump with excitement.

Colin turned his head to see the tail of the goat disappear forever. "You were right, Amy," he said, gathering up his coat. "What a confident goat."

"That animal has really opened my eyes. I feel empowered. I could do anything!"

Colin was busy scanning the tent, looking for Amy's mum. "That's nice, my dear," he replied with a slow yawn. "A good theatre show should always get you thinking about life's big questions."

Amy stood staring at where the animal had left. She had to find that goat. And for some reason she couldn't explain, she knew it wanted to be found.

3
Competitive cross country

The following morning, Amy's excitement had long disappeared.

"Get on with it, Amy! You lazy, *lazy* girl!" shouted Ms Trudy-Wudy, Amy's P.E. teacher. "You've got another three laps yet!" Globs of orange Jaffa Cake dropped from the woman's mouth as she barked orders in the rain.

The wind was angry today. It threw splatters of cold rain into Amy's face as she ran. And for the first time in her life, she was coming last. She usually loved cross country, the freedom of running through fields like a dog off the lead. Always beating her classmates, to finish in a satisfying, sweaty mess. But today wasn't like that.

This morning, Amy's mum had been running late for Circus Society so shoved Amy out of the house so quickly, she'd forgotten her trainers. Ms Trudy-Wudy didn't see this as a problem so forced Amy to run the full course in her cold, bare feet! This woman was obsessed with making everyone run. Be it on the toilet or standing in front of the class playing the recorder, if she caught you, she'd blow her whistle and get you running.

She blew her whistle. "For goodness sake, girl, *run* – everyone's waiting for you!" A heavy gust swept the last Jaffa Cake from her grasp.

The wind dragged Amy back. Her thin t-shirt clung around her body, working with the wind as she lifted her heavy feet in the mud.

"Yeah, get on with it, Amy-Wamey," came a mimicking voice behind her.

Amy stopped, wiping rain from her eyes to see where the voice came from. Suddenly her tummy tightened in fear.

Sarah and Sara were skipping towards her.

Like all bullies, Sarah and Sara had an art of always finding their victim. They loved hunting her out like it was a sport. Amy would nervously plan her route around the school corridors, avoiding certain places like the water fountain where they liked to hang out. But they always found her. Always waiting around a quiet corner.

"Did you know that you and your big buck teeth are coming last?" teased Sarah or Sara, it was difficult to tell who.

Not only were the girl's bullies, but they were also identical twin bullies with almost identical names. Amy could never tell them apart. (No one could).

"Since you came to our school, you haven't stopped banging on about how you're amazing at cross country," said Sara or Sarah.

Amy stared at the sisters, she turned her head back and forth, desperate to tell them apart. Splattered across their identical faces were identical freckles. They were so identical you could measure them by the degree with a protractor. Upon their heads were identical blonde bunches you could measure by the centimetre. Looking at them, they didn't fit the obvious bully 'mould' so teachers never noticed them teasing Amy. In fact, the teachers thought the three girls were best friends!

Tucked up in a warm hoody, Sarah glared at Amy in her thin t-shirt. "Did you understand what I just said?"

"I'm not sure she understands nothing," answered Sara.

Abruptly Sarah smacked her sister across the back of the head. "*Nothing*!? Not sure she understands *nothing*? That's terrible grammar, you used a double negative. Would you have spotted the mistake had I not highlighted it?"

Though the twins were rotten nasty girls, they were top of the class in every subject. Especially English. To most children, a confident reader with excellent spelling would seem uncool, but at this new posh school, it was as cool as they come.

Sara threw up her hands in defeat. "So what - no one cares! Stinky Amy-Wamey doesn't care. Do you?" asked Sara, staring straight at the shivering girl.

Amy opened her mouth but was too scared to speak. Her mind raced back to the goat at the circus and what it would do in this situation. She knew she should say something but Colin her stepdad always taught her not to rise to bullies (especially when she couldn't tell them apart).

Suddenly Sarah glanced down and spotted Amy's muddy, naked feet.

"OH MY GOSH LOOK AT THOSE HOBBIT FEET!" "Are you in bare feet!?" shouted the sister. "You are, aren't you!? Why aren't you wearing trainers!? Are you trying to be different again? Your big rabbit teeth already make you stand out so I wouldn't worry about it!"

The sisters threw back their heads and cackled loudly like a pair of pesky parrots. Embarrassed, Amy pushed her feet deep into the ground to hide them - but it only made them muddier. She'd slipped around the fields so much she'd splattered wet mud up her legs, down her arms and even on the tip of her nose.

"And she's been eating the mud," said Sara, pointing at the brown lump on Amy's nose.

Amy tried to inspect the mud on her face. In a panic, she wiped it away but with such muddy hands, she simply smeared it around her mouth. It's never good to agree with a bully but now it really did look like she'd been enjoying a bowl of mud porridge for breakfast.

"HAHAHAHAHA!" the bullies erupted.

"I- I can't get it off!" cried Amy. The more she panicked, the muddier she became.

Then, Amy saw the twins share a look. An evil smile stretched across their faces. It was the kind of smile nasty twin sisters share when they have a nasty twin sister idea.

"Hey Amy, stop. Don't worry about it," said Sarah softly like she was calming a caged bird. "Mud is really good for your skin. Our big sister *always* uses it. She piles it up on her face with bits of cucumber on her eyes. Isn't that right, Sis?"

"OHH absolutely," stressed Sara. "It gets rid of all her wrinkles."

"In fact, she puts it all over her body."

"Yeah, she likes to sit in a big bathtub of it when chatting on the phone to her silly boyfriend."

Amy stopped and listened to the girls. She slowly let out a breath of air. It felt like she'd been nervously holding her breath since Sarah and Sara found her.

"Really?" she asked hopefully.

"Of course!"

Amy allowed herself to relax. She suddenly felt less embarrassed as she stood freezing in front of the sisters.

"You must be freeeeeeezing," said Sara or Sarah, suddenly concerned.

"Yeah," said the other sister. "It wasn't cool for us to make fun of you, especially when you're so new to our school."

"We're *really* sorry. Let's hug it out." She opened her arms wide, welcoming the wind-swept girl in.

Amy hesitated for a moment. She was desperate to believe their words and desperate to make friends, so stepped into the hug.

"There we are," said Sarah, squeezing her tight.

Amy rested her face into the girl's soft jumper and for a few seconds felt protected. Protected from the wind and rain, protected from her parent's divorce and protected from this new school where she knew no one. But then, as she tried to leave the hug, she felt Sarah's grip tighten around her. The bully linked her fingers and locked her arms so tight around Amy, it was difficult for her to breathe.

"Sarah...I can't...breathe -"

Then, out of the corner of her eye, Amy saw the other twin sneak behind her. She was holding something.

Amy panicked at what was about to happen. "Let go of me!" she cried, trying to push away.

All at once, Amy felt her t-shirt collar yanked open and something wet sliding down her back.

Sarah quickly pushed the girl away and took a huge step back. "Phwoar! That stinks!"

"What is it!?" said Amy shaking her t-shirt. "What have you put down my back?" She was trying not to cry.

"Dog poo," said Sara proudly, wiping her hands on the wet grass.

After Sara said it, she could smell it. The *stench* of it. It filled Amy's nostrils and stung the back of her throat. Because it was on her body, she couldn't escape the toxic smell and the more she waved her arms to get away, the more the smell spread around her.

"We were only trying to help," continued Sara. "Dog poo is *even* better for you than mud, just not many people know about it."

"Yeah," continued the other twin in a squeaky voice as she held her nose. "In fact, why not have some for your hair!"

Sarah picked up a long thin twig to flick what remained at Amy. Seeing what was to happen, Amy spun around to make a run for it. She took one step but forgot she wasn't wearing any trainers, so slipped and fell flat in a puddle.

This time Sarah and Sara laughed so loudly Ms Trudy-Wudy heard.

"Why aren't you girls running!?" yelled Ms Trudy-Wudy from across the field. "Everyone must always be running - all the time!" She blew her whistle loudly to make a point.

The two girls didn't want the enormous woman to come over. She often sat on children as punishment.

"Poor Amy-Wamey, let me know if you need another big hug," said Sarah down at Amy on the ground, pretending to wipe away fake baby tears.

"Big baby! Wah wah wah"

Amy lifted her head from the muddy ground to watch them jump over a fence and slip to the front of the race. "Dirty cheaters," she said under her breath once the bullies were far enough away not to hear. She heaved herself up off the ground and shook each foot vigorously, sending heavy clumps of mud flying. "I hate this school, I *hate* it!"

Then at once, Amy sensed something dart behind her.

She froze.

It wasn't Sarah or Sara, they were long gone. And it couldn't be Ms Trudy-Wudy, she was too lazy to dart anywhere at such speed.

Amy cleared her dry throat and called out to the fields. "Hello…?"

The wind stole her cry. The tall trees moaned as they bent back unnaturally in the gale.

There was no reply.

"I'm just shaken up."

But suddenly, something darted back.

This time Amy felt it. She felt the hairs of something brush against the back of her arms.

Before she could do anything, there came an almighty cry.

"*Mehhhhhhhhhhhhhhhhhhh.*"

Amy spun around.

"I know that noise!"

Feeling suddenly confident, she darted to a small gap in the bushes where the noise came from. Being a lover of nature, she had no problem sticking her head into the bush to see the other side. The cry came again, delivered by the wind.

"*Mehhhhhhhhhhhh.*"

"I know what it is!" said Amy, pulling her head back out, along with a couple of leaves.

But before she had a chance to speak, in

bounced the goat from the circus. Despite it also being covered in mud, the single white line of fur was still visible across its back. Plus, it was still wearing Norman's hat!

"It's you!" cried Amy as if greeting an old friend.

"*Mehhhhhh*," replied the animal, darting away on long scrawny legs, just like Amy's.

"No, wait!"

The goat turned back and stared with its large, marble-green eyes. It stamped its hooves heavy with mud. On one hoof it was wearing an old shoe.

"You want me to follow you?" asked Amy.

The goat nodded.

"I've never followed a goat before."

The animal looked at the girl as if to say, *and your point is?*

Amy glanced round to where she thought Ms Trudy-Wudy and her classmates were. Without realising it, she had wandered far from the school gates.

"I have to go back," she said. "I can't be out of bounds, it's rule number 732 in the School Rules Handbook."

And she was absolutely right, getting caught out of bounds meant instant, yes instant expulsion. Everyone, however new to the school knew this rule.

The goat rolled its big eyes in a "*You're like totally wasting my time*" kind of way.

"No, don't look at me like that," said Amy, feeling comfortable enough around the animal to answer back like she usually would.

As she wrestled thinking of what to do, she felt the mud on her legs harden. The air warmed around her as the sun came out. She had to make a decision quickly. The goat was already trotting away.

She could re-join her class and make it back just in time for History. Or she could follow the goat and risk being expelled from the school she hated. She looked over her shoulder to check no one was watching, then followed the animal.

4
Goat noises

The sound a goat makes is unlike any other animal. They extend their long necks, curl back their pointy tongues and let out an almighty cry. It starts flat then wavers up and down like a rusty clarinet being played by someone with no teeth.

When Amy first heard this noise, she knew it at once. Her ears pricked up and she felt like she was being called by one of her own.

Through the bushes, Amy blindly followed her new friend. Tiny twigs grazed her arms, leaving light scratches. Hanging branches pulled at her messy bun. All the while Amy didn't notice, she was too excited to see where they were going.

At once the goat stopped, causing Amy to smack into its hind legs.

'*Mehhhhhhhhhhh!*' it bleated in Amy's face, blowing her long fringe from her eyes.

"Oh my," spluttered Amy, choking on the animal's bad breath.

It shuffled closer to Amy and took a hungry bite out of her t-shirt. Its wonky square teeth looked like the keys of a broken keyboard.

"Don't chew that! Mother won't be happy buying another one."

To avoid ripping her gym wear and explaining the animal bite mark (could she blame it on her brother, Sebastián?) she had no choice but to be pulled along by the animal. It was desperate to show her something.

This new route was not made for humans. There

were stinging nettles and brambles everywhere.

They surrounded her, arching over her like a tunnel and reaching down, trying to grab her. Poor Amy with her long limbs was struggling to keep up.

"Please slow down!" she called ahead to the animal, who started bouncing up and down like an uncontrollable pogo stick.

But then, between a small parting of tangled brambles, the goat stopped. Amy wasn't ready for what happened next.

The goat nuzzled the nettles, using its large top hat to clear a gap for her. Crouched low on her hands and knees to peek through the parting, Amy stared out.

Ahead of her was a field. A very large field. The field was the size of three football pitches and there was a giant water slide running through it, as well as a smart coffee bar, and a bowling alley.

Amy rubbed her eyes like a cartoon trying to believe the sight. She blinked a few times and continued to see amazing things in this field, like a library of books and someone very hairy flying in the air on a trampoline. And then, suddenly she saw it.

Goats. Hundreds, no, THOUSANDS of them. Everywhere. Like a swarm of locusts, they covered the area so thickly Amy could barely see the grass. It looked as if every single goat was different. Unique in size, breed, shape and colour. And what's more, they appeared to be doing things one wouldn't expect a goat to do. No, they were doing things one wouldn't *believe* a goat could do.

"*Mehhhhhhh*," cried the goat from the circus beside her.

"I don't understand," whispered Amy. "Where are we?" She stared out like she'd been hypnotised by a magician.

Ignoring her question, the goat trotted happily into the field. Amy followed at once. They pushed their way through the goat crowds like it was a busy London underground station. The goat from the circus had a white tip on its high tail Amy could spot when feeling lost. She followed slowly, her head twisting and turning to see everything. Her mouth hung open in shock.

First, they passed two nanny goats wearing flowery dresses. They were human dresses, not dresses designed for stumpy goats. The animals had their skinny front hooves poked through the sleeves. Amy looked with the rest of the dress in the mud.

When they walked, their wobbly pink udders poked out.

Next, they passed a very serious long-haired goat with curly horns. He was sitting in a foldable beach chair reading a book titled 'Structural Mass Spectrometry: Volume 2', a *very* smart book. He sat like a human, holding the hardback cover between his hooves. Once he'd finished reading a page, instead of turning it over, he ate it. He nibbled the corner with his large teeth then ripped the whole thing out down the spine. Amy was less surprised by this than the goats in dresses, as goats are known to chew everything.

Then, over by a large hay bale, Amy saw the most peculiar thing yet. Like everyone her age, Amy wondered if animals could talk. Here was her answer. From where she stood, she could see an old goat teacher with a very long white beard standing in front of a row of goat students. The teacher was holding a Goat-to-French-Translation-Dictionary.

Slightly struggling with her clunky hooves, the goat teacher opened a page, prodded at a picture of a lamp shade and in the most fluent of French uttered, "*Abat-jour.*"

The small kid goats stared up at their teacher and repeated, "*Abat-jour.*" They spoke it perfectly like a class of children at a very expensive British boarding school.

Upon hearing this Amy stopped in her tracks.

"Lamp shade!?" she blurted without thinking. "Why on earth would a goat need to know the word *lamp shade*?"

Being a bright and open-minded girl, upon seeing goats wearing dresses, playing with slime and getting in a muddle with Twister (more on that later) Amy realised what she found most peculiar was not that she had discovered, for the first time in history, animals speaking, and not that, once again for the first time in history, she had discovered animals speaking *French*; but what she found *most* outrageous and *most* alarming and *most* slap-in-the-face-shocking was their decision to learn the word *LAMP SHADE*!!!

"I don't know if I fully agree with the learning of that word," she blurted to the goat teacher. "Why don't you learn something more useful that goats use every day? And why are you learning it in French? None of it makes sense."

The goat from the circus turned around to her "*Soyez silencieux!*" it snapped, in a far better accent than Amy could do. "*Nous apprenons ce que nous voulons!*"

Amy had no idea what the goat had said but she felt it was along the lines of 'mind your own business and pipe down!'

Continuing the tour in the sun, something slowly dawned on Amy. There were no rules. Unlike her life which was FULL of rules at school and home. These goats did what they wanted, when they wanted. There were no stressy parents or teachers barking, "Stop doing that!" Or, "Choose one or the other!" These goats were doing anything, and it

didn't matter if it made sense. Amy had never seen anything like it. Some goats were doing 'human' things like sat scrolling on their phones, or putting on lipstick, whereas others were doing 'goat' things, like having a good scratch against a tree stump. In fact, on closer look, some were doing a mix like playing Monopoly, while having a good scratch against a tree stump. Feeling brave, Amy stopped following the goat from the circus to explore on her own. The birds were singing happily and despite the strong smell of poo, she felt confident. She wiggled her way through the crowd to find three young kid goats standing on their back legs, jumping over a skipping rope. There were two on either end twirling the rope, and a very bouncy one in the middle, springing hoof to hoof to head to hoof.

"Why hello there. My name's Amy, what a cool place this is and…"

She rambled on before pausing mid-sentence, remembering they had been speaking French. Being a proud English-speaking Brit, Amy's stepdad, Colin, told her to not bother learning French. Everyone who speaks French will learn English, he liked to say. But look what good that advice turned out to be, as now she knew none!

"Err, *Bonjour, je m'appelle* Amy and it is nice to meet you," she attempted. She spoke the English words in a heavy French accent.

One of the small kid goats turning the rope smiled up at the girl. "*Bonjour!*"

Amy felt her heart leap. "Oh, *Bonjour!*" she squealed with delight over her first French conversation (forgetting it had been with a goat). Just as she opened her mouth to continue, the small animal spoke again.

"*Mehhhhhhhh.*"

Amy couldn't stop her face from falling. "Why have you stopped speaking French? That doesn't make any sense," She protested down at the animal. "If you start speaking French, you can't just switch when you feel like it."

Quickly she threw her hands over her mouth to stop more words from falling out. She couldn't believe she'd just said that! She sounded like her mum! Who was *she* to tell this goat what to do!? The goats were clearly offended. They'd stopped their fun skipping game to turn and stare at the girl.

Unsure how to apologise Amy quickly opened her mouth wide, filled her lungs and cried out.

"*Mehhhhhhhh!*"

The young kid goats jumped for joy at Amy's goat noise. Across the field, the goat from the circus heard Amy's cry and bounced over. It proudly nuzzled its large head into Amy's back.

"I sounded just like a goat, didn't I!?" cried Amy, suddenly impressed with herself.

Spotting a large hay bale, the goat clambered onto it and nodded its head for Amy to follow.

"Me?" asked Amy, pointing at herself.

"*Oui,*" said the animal in French.

Without hesitation, Amy grabbed the scratchy

34

hay bale and pulled herself up. Her muddy, bare feet dangled over the edge as she looked out at this new life. She felt a gentle breeze tickle her neck. Throughout the afternoon her excitement had grown and grown like a birthday balloon being pumped full of air.

The goat from the circus parked itself upon Amy's ap like a well-trained dog.

"Oh pong," blurted Amy, crushed by its weight. "You stink!"

The goat glared up at Amy. It curled its wide nostrils to imply that Amy smelt no better.

"Me!? But I smell of flowers," replied Amy, lifting her arm to have a good sniff. She winced back in shock. "Phwoar! You're right!"

Amy had spent all afternoon with the animals and only now realised she was covered in mud, stinking of goat. She spat in her hands, rubbed them together and smoothed down her hair and fringe. "Mum won't like me smelling when I get home," she giggled to herself.

Suddenly, upon hearing her own words, she was drenched with panic. The sun was quickly setting and she should have been home hours ago. She'd missed the rest of school plus her evening pogo stick lesson Mum forced her to attend. The magic of the day was gone.

"I have to go!" She cried, pushing the goat off. She jumped down from the spikey hay bale. Mum would be home from circus training any second and Amy had to be home and washed before her, otherwise, she'd be caught.

Amy sprinted through the stinging nettles, back

the way she came. "Goodbye and thank you!" she shouted over her shoulder as the goat stared, confused.

As she ran, she couldn't help but wonder if she'd seen Mrs Moopleton, the headmistress, watching her from the school window.

5
Oh, pong!

"I mustn't panic," said Amy, bent over between gasps. On the driveway sat her Mum's car. Amy could feel the engine heat rising from it. This meant she'd just arrived and would be hunting the house for her. Amy tried to swallow but her throat was too dry. She didn't know if it was the sprint home, or because she could hear her mum shouting her name in the house.

Tiptoeing to the wooden side gate, she slowly pushed it open. It squealed in protest, causing Amy to freeze and grit her teeth. She leant into it again. Keeping her head low she slipped into the garden - and instantly saw her stepdad.

He was giving Stewart the cat a lavish bubble bath in the inflatable paddling pool. Every evening in the garden he gave the cat a good wash to help tackle his allergies. Only recently Mum made him do it in the garden, away from her fancy bath soaps.

"Oh, heavens!" yelped Colin as he spotted his muddy stepdaughter. "You almost gave me a heart *a-a-a-achooooooo!*"

Amy watched him erupt with sneezes. He was bent over the cat wearing a face mask and long yellow gloves past his elbows. To anyone who didn't know him, they'd think he was disposing of highly toxic waste, not massaging bubbles into a fluffy pussy cat.

"You made me jump out my skin *a-a-achooooooo!*" he sneezed again, this time steaming up his mask.

"Meeeeeooowwww!" shrieked a soggy Stewart the cat. Normally Stewart enjoyed these pampering sessions but right now he had a screwed-up nose, angry with the invasion of privacy.

Amy bent low to the ground as she walked. Careful not to be spotted from inside. She could see that the heat from the oven and her Mother's shouts had steamed up the kitchen windows.

"Shhhhhh, Colin. Mum will hear you and then I'll get it in the neck."

Colin lifted his mask and wrinkled his nose. "There's some kind of smell on you, Amy. I mean, more than usual. What type of school do your parents send you to?"

Amy avoided eye contact. "Oh, it's nothing. It's just from cross country, you pick up all kinds of things."

"*Achooooooo*! Is that so?" he said suspiciously, eyeing her up. Amy looked away suddenly very interested in the house's brickwork.

"It seems you've picked up something I'm heavily allergic to," he continued, blowing his nose into a wet hankie. "Into the paddling pool with the cat, I can't have you making me sneeze all evening."

"What!? No way!"

"Now I know you don't like washing Amy -"

"It's not that. I'll go have a shower inside, without the cat... like a normal person!"

Amy made a lunge for the backdoor.

"Not one more smelly step," said Colin, scooping her up around the waist. "You stink like a farmyard animal. You'll infect the whole house and I'll be up coughing and spluttering all night. And what would your Mother say, having you sneak in at this time of night?"

Amy stopped squealing; he had her there. She'd hoped Colin would be so distracted with washing her, he wouldn't notice the time.

"Didn't think I'd notice the time, did you?" he said arching a bushy eyebrow with a cheeky smile.

"Well, I just thought -" she mumbled when suddenly, she was sprayed in the face with the garden hose.

"Got ya!"

"Oh no, that's f-f-freezing!"

"Ha! That'll teach you, you pongy girl!" Colin laughed loudly as he soaked the girl head to toe like he was simply watering the strawberry bushes.

Despite his unusual methods of getting Amy to wash, Colin's parenting was spot on. Having joined Amy's family a few months ago when he started dating Amy's mum, he took to parenting very well. Whenever Amy was upset about the bullies at her new school, he always turned off the vacuum and listened.

All at once, Mum stuck her long neck out the small kitchen window to give them both a good telling-off.

"So, this is where the pair of you are hiding! I come back from circus training, where I almost succeeded in balancing on my head while riding a camel and find myself searching the house for the pair of you – and you're out here mucking around with the blasted garden hose!"

Amy and Colin sheepishly looked up at the woman as they stood dripping with water. Her face was thick with show makeup from rehearsal - her purple eyeshadow and red cheeks made her look like a clown.

"Well!?" she barked. Her mouth looked wider than normal thanks to the deep red lipstick. "Have you been out here this whole time, Amy?"

"I...um...."

"Yes. She's been out here with me all evening," interrupted Colin, nudging Amy in the back with the hose nozzle. "She came home the moment school finished."

"Well I know that's a lie," said Mum, flapping her thick black eyelashes.

Amy turned to Colin, searching his eyes in panic.

"Because Amy has been at her pogo stick class tonight," she continued. "She's been learning useful pogo stick skills that will help shape her future. I assume that's why you smell so ghastly, Amy?"

"I, um - " continued Amy uselessly.

"Yes, that's right!" said Colin, winking at his stepdaughter, happy to play along with the small fib. "She came straight home after pingo step, no...*pogo stick* training. That's why I'm giving her a good hose down in the garden, as all that jumping has made the girl stink!"

"Good idea!" Mum nodded. "Nothing worse than owning smelly children. What would the members of my clarinet band say about that? Once you're clean, in you come. Clever Sebastián has made us a glorious dinner."

And with that, her head retracted, and the window slammed shut. Amy and Colin stood silently, shivering in their soggy clothes. Through the wall, they could hear a muffled moan about Mum's fancy bath soaps. Feeling uncomfortable, Amy turned to her stepdad and gave him a big hug around his waist. Her fingertips couldn't meet when she reached around his belly.

"Thanks, Colin," she mumbled into his soggy jumper.

"Not a problem. I don't blame you for not wanting to go to pingo stomp classes - "

"*Pogo* stick."

"Yes, that too." He released the girl's grip and bent down close so their eyes were level. "But do promise me you'll never lie about your whereabouts again, Amy?"

This was the first time Colin had spoken to Amy so seriously. She didn't know where to look so she focused on the little indent on his chubby chin. "Okay," she lied, knowing he would never accept her wanting to be like a goat.

Colin ruffled her hair like a wet dog. Taking her

small hand, he led her inside. As they pushed open the back door, an array of mouth-watering smells filled their bodies. Amy felt the goose pimples on her arms smooth out in the warm kitchen.

She bent down and looked through the glass panel of the oven. There was a tinfoil-wrapped meat joint roasting away, dribbling in fat. On the hob sprouts spluttered in steam. And in the centre of the kitchen table was Amy's favourite, piles of roast potatoes with crispy edges. In the evenings Sebastián didn't have cheerleading practice, he cooked up feasts better than any dinner lady at school.

"Sit down, sit down everyone," said Mum, pulling out chairs around the table. "Don't sit on a stool Amy, sit on a proper chair."

Amy rolled her eyes and dragged over a 'proper' chair.

"You've not set me a place," snapped Amy to Sebastián. He ignored her, disappearing in a puff of steam as he drained the carrots.

Mum looked Amy up and down. "Aren't you going to change first, Amy?"

Amy stared down at herself. Colin had missed some mud on her knees which was starting to harden and crumble all over the floor. "Why does it matter?"

"Because it's dinner time and it's important to look smart."

Amy ignored her, leaning forward to grab a fork. Quickly Amy realised Mum was in one of her telling-off moods so whatever she did, she'd be told off.

This would never happen in the Goat Kingdom, Amy thought to herself, behind gritted teeth.

"Amy, are you deliberately holding your knife and

42

fork incorrectly?" continued Mum, plonking a steaming potato in her mouth. "I'll book an etiquette class for tomorrow, after your trumpet lesson." She spluttered potato over the table as she spoke.

Amy flicked the clump of chewed potato off her cheek. She inhaled deeply. She could feel herself getting angry. Very angry. She felt the thump of her heart quicken. She was trying not to listen but could hear Mum squawking on about Amy's messy hair. Why wasn't Colin standing up for her?

She'd had enough. She knew if Mum commented on her actions one more time, she'd explode the way baboons do when they rip people's faces off!

And then it happened.

"Amy," said Mum, not looking up. "Could I bother you to pass the salt - "

"SHUT UP, MUM! JUST SHUT UP!"

Colin jumped, dropping his fork with a clatter. Sebastián jumped, dropping a pan with a thud. Everyone turned to stare at this angry little girl.

She'd cracked.

There's no other way to say it.

And it was all due to her mum telling her what to do. *Always* telling her what to do. As a fully grown 10-year-old, shouldn't Amy be allowed to make her own decision about how she holds her knife and fork? Well, apparently not in her Mum's eyes. If she were a goat in the Goat Kingdom, she'd never be told what to do.

Mum slowly rose from the kitchen table like she was Queen Victoria herself.

"Well, in all my years parenting you children," she whispered to the still room. "I have never heard

43

such vulgarity at the dinner table. And to think, I give you so much with violin lessons and extra tutoring. I was even going to send you to a class about how to properly rinse out recyclable cans - but no! I won't - "

"That's exactly my point, Mum!" interrupted Amy. Colin hid his face in his hands. "You won't let me do anything *I* want to do! I have to do *everything* you say, *all* the time. It's like you're trying to brainwash me into this perfect, boring person - just like you!"

At this comment, Amy's mother inhaled slowly and deeply.

"Off to your room!" she erupted like she was sending her own daughter to be beheaded at the Tower of London.

With both arms Amy shoved her chair from the table, screeching it across the floor. She ignored Colin's eyes as she marched upstairs. Stomp, stomp, stomping until she slammed her bedroom door shut, shaking the whole house. She flung herself on the bed, pushing the pillows onto the floor.

She chucked one across the room to watch it splat and slide down the front of her wardrobe.

She knew she was acting like a baby but couldn't help it. She took a deep breath in. Slowly her shoulders and neck started to relax. She noticed her hands were in tight fists so shook them out. As she lay in her silent room with the sound of chatter drifting up, she realised she wasn't sad. She felt the opposite. She was proud. Just one visit to the goat pen had taught her so much about being herself, and most importantly, standing up for herself.

She was also relieved she hadn't eaten dinner. Later that evening Colin came upstairs to check on her with a plate of cold food. She sniffed the slice of meat to discover it was goat! She couldn't eat one of her own. That's how she felt now. As she sat chewing a soggy potato that was no longer crispy around the edges, she realised something. She wanted to visit the goats again. She had to. But first, she had to get through a school day of being sensible and un-goat-like.

Or maybe not…

6
Expressing your inner goat-ness

The next day at school Amy wanted to misbehave. She'd woken up with a fire of naughtiness burning in her belly. She dressed at top speed, knowing the only way to put out this fire was to act like a goat at school. This didn't mean tearing down the corridor or biting anyone who stroked her. No, she wanted to be far more secretive. She wanted to slip goat actions into her day without getting caught. It was called 'expressing her inner goat-ness'. This could be crying *mehhhhh* like a goat when someone called her name. Or chewing the bottom of someone's coat as it hung off the back of their chair. Keen to try out her new life, her first attempt was morning registration.

Mr McSporran, Amy's burly Scottish form tutor, smashed into the classroom in his usual way. He was a tall, well-built man with bulging arms. Adults gossiped that he used his two young sons as weights. One hanging off each arm, lifting them as he did squats.

"Haud yer wheesht - a'm reading yer names 'n' respond wi' aye!" he bellowed to the class.

Before he'd walked in, the children had been treating the classroom like a jungle gym: jumping across the desks and crawling under the chairs. But now they'd shot to attention. Their shiny, alert eyes stared up at the man.

"Guid, let's git gaun'," he said, clambering behind his desk. He leant over to the drawer and yanked it

46

open so hard the handle came off in his hand. He threw it to the side and took out the heavy registration book. He slammed the drawer shut making the desk jump like a nervous donkey. "Right now - Oscar Ablebottom, ye 'ere?"

Oscar's head shot up. "Yes, Sir. Here."

"Aye," replied Mr Sporran, not looking at the boy. "Chloe Bassingthwaighte?"

"Yes, Sir."

Amy sat chewing the end of her pencil, nervous about her name being called. She wasn't scared thinking about how Mr McSporran could probably crush her with his left thumb. But instead nervous about what she had planned when -

"Amy Bloomsy?"

"Mehhhhhh."

"Sabrina Burki?"

"Yes, Sir."

And there it was! Blink and it would go missed! Not a single classmate had noticed Amy answer, *'mehhh'* to her name. Amy felt a huge smile grow across her face. Quickly she darted her eyes down to avoid being caught. She didn't know if she'd imagined it, but she thought she saw Sara the bully glare at her when she mehhhhed like a goat.

Once the register had finished, the children gathered their books and bags for Geography class. Amy jumped up quickly, tripping over her bag strap. Sara and Sarah, the identical twins with almost identical names, stood whispering and pointing at her. They had noticed something different about her.

"Excuse me, sorry - " murmured Amy as she squeezed through everyone to leave the room first.

Expressing her goat-ness in front of Miss Hamm, the Geography teacher would be easy. Miss Hamm was deaf, always had her eyes closed and smelt of warm butter. Unsurprisingly, she never noticed or heard a single thing. Students could stand at the front of the classroom wearing flippers and blowing a big trumpet and she wouldn't bat an eyelid. Instead, she'd continue thinking she was pointing to Italy on the map when it was actually Uzbekistan.

Feeling confident, Amy skipped into the classroom. She pulled out a chair from a desk in the front room, directly under the teacher's nose. She wanted to add some risk. With books ready and open, she glanced up expecting to see Miss Hamm talking to a wall but was instead met by a stranger.

"Take out your books and turn to page 15."

Amy stared up at the woman. She was young for a teacher, around 24, and was wearing smart grey shoes and a smart grey suit. She wasn't smiling. Her face wasn't showing any expression but at the same time, she looked alert and hard-working. Amy had a terrible feeling that no matter how hard she tried, she'd leave this woman's class having learnt something.

"Something you wish to share with the class?" she hissed to Oscar and Sabrina. The whole class turned and gawked at the pair yapping away.

"Naaaa thanks," replied Oscar, not looking up.

Suddenly a white piece of chalk flew across the room hitting Oscar on the nose and leaving a dusty white mark.

"No thank you, Miss Jäger-Pfeiffer," the woman corrected, fingering a fresh piece of chalk.

Like a magic spell, Oscar was instantly disciplined, "No thank you, Miss Jäger-Pfeiffer. I apologise."

"Good. Because taking out your textbook and turning to page 15 does not require a conversation with the person sat next to you."

Amy gulped nervously. This was one of those really good teachers who felt it important to have control over the class. How was she going to get away with her goat-ness now, she thought?

Miss Jäger-Pfeiffer stood directly in front of Amy's desk as if she sensed the girl's misbehaving thoughts. Amy held her breath. The woman's perfume was strong and bringing on a headache. Amy's body was too tight to breathe normally.

"Miss Hamm could not make today's class," said Miss Jäger-Pfeiffer, leaning forward onto Amy's desk as she addressed the room. "So, I am your substitute teacher for the day. I want you to take 10 minutes to complete the first four source questions at the bottom corner of the page. This exercise does not require a group discussion."

Amy stared down at the questions in her book. Miss Hamm usually set these four questions to take the entire lesson, not the first 10 minutes! She glanced over her shoulder, expecting one of the twins to say this as they loved to correct teachers. But to her shock, everyone had their heads down, scribbling away.

Amy looked back at the open book. The first question was about river erosion, a very dull topic. Amy felt her eyes watering as she yawned widely into her hand. She stared at the text, reading the same question over and over but it wasn't going in. She was daydreaming about goats. They'd be so disappointed to know Amy hadn't acted like a goat because it was more difficult than she'd first thought. She had to at least try.

And so, while everyone's heads were down, Amy stuck hers up like an ostrich, searching for something goaty to do. Miss Jäger-Pfeiffer spotted her instantly and snatched up a piece of chalk. She held it above her head, like a warning sign, ready to throw. Amy sunk back down to her textbook, burying her face in it.

Suddenly, with the book so close to her face it gave her an idea, and it was not Geography related. She remembered back to the Goat Kingdom and the clever goat reading the physics book. It had stopped occasionally to chew a page. Chewing school textbooks would count as damage to school property, (rule number 231 in the school handbook) but Amy was getting desperate.

She stared at the book in front of her, there were two corners to choose from. The corner of page 16 was laminated in plastic. This meant it would be thick, so tricky to tear with human teeth. Whereas, on the opposite page, page 15, the laminate had come apart, exposing the paper. Much easier. However, if Amy ripped, chewed and swallowed the corner of this page, she would be eating the questions Miss Jäger-Pfeiffer had just set.

Amy lowered her head so close to the corner of page 15 it looked like she'd fallen asleep on her face. She gave the book a good sniff.

"Yuck," she whispered under her breath. "Smells like Colin's gardening socks."

But Amy knew if she wanted to be like her new goat friends, she couldn't find germs off-putting. So, ever so quietly, she poked out the tip of her tongue and licked the page. Then, with a bit more spit she licked a bigger bit. Before she realised it, she was tearing at the edge with her big front teeth.

RIIIIIIP went the page in the deathly silent classroom.

Miss Jäger-Pfeiffer jumped at once. She inspected the children like a spy surveillance camera on a submarine. Amy froze. Inside her mouth was a piece of the textbook. Saliva quickly moistened the paper and to her surprise, she found it rather tasty. Then, without thinking about it she swallowed the paper. Instantly, she fancied another bite. So, she ripped off a second bit and ate it. Then a little bit more. For the first time in her life she felt proud of her big front teeth because before she knew it, she had gobbled the whole of page 15 and was sniffing out pages 16 to 17.

When the school bell finally rang, Amy was so full of paper that she didn't fancy her packed lunch. She was also bursting to the brim, excited to tell her goat friends what she'd done. Outside in the fresh air, she swiftly left the school grounds to the Goat Kingdom. She knew she'd made it when the smell of stale goat poo filled her nostrils.

"*Mehhhhhhhhhhhh,*" cried the goat from the circus upon seeing Amy clamber through the nettles.

"Hello -I - so much to tell you..." Amy puffed out of breath, ignoring the throbbing red stings up her arm. "And then – you wouldn't quite believe it! Ripped it with my teeth!" Amy flung her arms around and then stopped, pointing at her two large front teeth.

A small ginger dwarf goat with long curly hair strolled up to Amy. It was walking on its back legs, holding a flowery tea tray.

"Oh, yes please," smiled Amy down at the animal, catching her breath. She sat on a pile of leaves and picked up a cup of steaming Earl Grey tea. Amy was learning that goats love Earl Grey.

The goat from the circus sat next to Amy, nibbling a ginger nut biscuit. Now both ready with tea, the goat nodded for Amy to continue. The girl launched into her story about this morning.

She rambled on to the animal, then stopped quite suddenly. She took a sip of tea and said, "You know, I don't even know your name?"

The goat stuck out its long, pink tongue.

"How very rude," said Amy, plonking a Custard Cream in her mouth. "After that, I definitely don't think you have a sensible name like Jane or Penelope." She continued with a full mouth, crumbs falling as she spoke. "Jane's and Penelope's don't go around sticking out their tongues to people."

The goat raised its teacup in agreement.

"Maybe you have an old-fashioned name like Ingrid?"

"*Non, non, non,*" protested the goat in French.

Amy scratched her head and swallowed. "Do you even have a name?"

The animal's large marble eyes looked blankly at the girl.

"Well, we can make one up for you!"

With this suggestion, the goat leapt up. It accidentally smashed the teapot with its back hoof as it bounced around excitedly.

"Excellent!" said Amy, ignoring the mess. "Now, you certainly don't fit the mould of a normal name as you're anything but normal." She stood up, wiping crumbs from her trousers. "The only odd name I can think of is Pocahontas - but you look nothing like her. Plus you're fluent in French so I feel like it should be a bit French. How about something like…Ôuhlet?"

The goat's nostrils flared.

"Okay, fine," she hushed, continuing to walk in circles around the goat as she thought out loud. "Maybe something more exciting that still sounds French. And it needs to be fun to pronounce. Um, Óhgloo, Ogli, Õogly - "

"*Mehhhhhhhhhhhh*!" the goat cried in excitement, jumping up like a game of Buckaroo.

"Õogly?!" repeated Amy excited.

"*Oui*! Õogly!"

Amy bent down and hugged the goat around its long neck. "Õogly," she said, sneaking the last Custard Cream. "It's the perfect name for my best friend."

7
Top grades

Amy could hardly believe it when she realised she'd been visiting the Goat Kingdom for over a month. Perhaps it was because she was now happy. Every day she acted like a goat, and every day she visited Õogly at the Goat Kingdom. She'd felt happier in these last few weeks than her whole life put together.

At school, Amy's goat-ness had quickly become normal. The teachers said she was the most disruptive student to have ever attended St Andrews School of Controlled Excellence & Unoriginality.

This title was first given to her by Mrs Moopleton, who'd towered over her, clutching a dripping grey paint brush and hissed, "You are the most disruptive student to have ever attended St Andrews School of Controlled Excellence & Unoriginality."

Amy wore this title with pride. Because it was true. No class, lunch break or sports lesson passed without acting like a goat. Last Thursday at a netball match against a rival school, Amy kept headbutting the other team.

"Keep running!" bellowed Ms Trudy-Wudy the PE teacher, oblivious to the children crying their eyes out.

Soon the other team were too scared to touch the ball so stood staring at it until the final whistle came. Amy's school won that match with 184 goals to 2, their best score yet!

Another time in the school canteen Amy leapt onto the lunch table, trotting up and down the rows. Plastic glasses of sugary apple juice toppled over, getting everyone wet. A bowl of yellow custard fell splat on Sebastián's lap. He'd shared a mean look with Sara and Sarah the identical twins with almost identical names who were also dripping in custard. Amy was enjoying herself too much. She didn't notice the mood darken.

"Because I'm so disruptive with my goat-ness," said Amy one break time, reporting back to the goats, "I'm forced to sit at the front of every classroom on a single desk called The Naughty Desk. But it's quite wonderful because being at the front means my grades have vastly improved. I'm top of the class in *every* subject!"

Oogly and the goats sat chewing bits of straw, eyes glued to the girl the way teenagers are glued to their phones. Amy explained how French was now her best subject, thanks to them. She could hold full conversations in the language with Madame Papillon, her French teacher. Often Amy brought the chat back to udders and food pellets, but it was all in perfect French. In Amy's report card, Madame Papillon had written:

'Incredibly bright student. At times disruptive when she crawls on all fours and eats classmates' pencil cases.'

Despite Amy's new ways, all the other children carried on as normal. Yes, some were irked by Amy's new behaviour. But the fear of being painted grey by Mrs Moopleton stopped them from also acting out. This made Amy sad as she knew her classmates would be happier if they could join her and be themselves.

The twins, however, felt differently. Before Amy joined *their* school, Sarah and Sara were joint top in every subject. The school hallways had been filled with their perfect schoolwork. Superb essays and sketches had been pinned to the cork boards that lined the corridors. But now their work could barely be seen. Buried beneath Amy's perfect French essays, you had to dig two or three layers down to catch just a glimpse of their maths test.

"What are we going to do!?" moaned Sara to Sarah one break time. They were leaning against the water fountain, staring up at the hallway plastered with Amy Bloomsy's name.

Sarah never heard her sister. Her mind was busy running through the evil trap she already had in place....

* * *

"Õogly! I'm here!" called Amy, trotting towards the Goat Kingdom.

It was a drizzly Monday lunchtime, and like every lunchtime, Amy had snuck off to visit her goat friends. "I've got 30 minutes before I've got to be back for Biology," continued Amy, speaking loudly. She assumed Õogly could hear her through the bushes, like always.

Amy knelt in the mud, ready to push back the stinging nettles - but stopped. The usual tangle of branches wasn't there. She looked down and saw a cut branch lying in the dirt. It looked like a gardener had used a saw to cut a perfect opening into the Goat Kingdom.

She picked up a piece of nettle and started chewing it. "Guess the goats were just sick of getting stung," she shrugged.

She glanced up to continue - but stopped. Suddenly she felt the need to stay very still. And listen. Her ears seemed sharper than usual. Picking up every crunch of leaf, snap of twig. She felt like a wild deer, listening out for the footsteps of a hunter. Just outside the Goat Kingdom, Amy would normally hear the goats laughing or playing the saxophone. But it was silent. The only sound was the light pitter patter of rain.

Amy glanced over her shoulder. No one was there. She was already on her hands and knees but

58

bent lower to the ground. She stepped carefully, avoiding the bits of cut nettle as if they were land mines. Inside the Goat Kingdom, she couldn't believe what she saw. Normally it looked like a messy playroom with recorders, skipping ropes and board games sprawled across the grass. But today was different. And that scared her.

It was empty.

Amy's stomach tightened. Her eyes darted from tree to Twister to food trough. The trough was full of untouched pellets. They were getting soggy in the rain.

"Õogly?" she asked quietly to the empty space.

At once a feeble goat cry sounded behind her. She spun round. In the far corner of the furthest field, she saw the grey and brown coats of goats. They were huddled together, shaking with fear.

"I don't understand," said Amy quietly.

"Don't understand what?" came a sinister voice.

Amy jumped at the sound of a human voice. She instantly recognised it.

Standing behind her were the twins. And in the middle of them, Sebastián.

"You've been caught."

8
"You've been caught."

"What's your bright idea now, Amy-Wamey?" teased Sarah. "Ask your freak farm friends how to avoid being expelled?" She twirled the end of her hair in her fingertips to show she really didn't care what happened to Amy.

But for Amy, this was the end. She'd been caught leaving the school grounds. She was going to be expelled from school. Her mind started to race: making a plan – panicking – jumping to a different plan.

Sebastián exhaled strongly like he was bored. Even now, he didn't talk or look at his sister. "Sarah, can you tell Amy how Mum will be utterly beside herself when I tell her she's not been going to her Monkey Drawing classes because she's hanging out with dirty goats."

Amy's head snapped up. How did he know that?

"Oh, look she didn't know?" he laughed with the bullies, ignoring Amy's stare. "Did she really think this was the first time we've seen her here?"

Sara pulled a camera out of her school bag. "Durrrr," she spat, waving the camera in Amy's face. "Your mum paid good money for those classes," she continued.

Amy frowned, not following.

"Monkey Drawing classes! I'm going to force you to draw a monkey in front of your Mum to prove you haven't been going."

Monkey Drawing classes were exactly what they sounded like: a class where you learnt how to draw various species of monkey. Amy cared very little about how to draw a monkey or why the class focused *only* on monkeys. But she did care about

Mum finding out she hadn't been going. First her pogo stick class, now this. She'd be furious.

"You wouldn't!" Amy snapped back, looking between her brother and the bullies.

"Try and stop us."

Sarah marched up to Amy and shoved her hard in the shoulder. "You've got nowhere to hide now."

Amy fell back. Sarah was a lot stronger than her. They both were. If it came down to a fight Amy would never beat them *and* Sebastián.

Quickly, Amy's eyes darted to the goats. They were cowering under a large tree in the corner of the field. Õogly was standing firmly at the front. Head and hat held high, she wasn't scared. Amy and Õogly's eyes locked. They knew -

"GRAB HER!" shouted Sarah.

The twins launched at Amy. They opened their arms wide, surrounding her like she was a nervous animal that could dart away. Sebastián combed his fingers through his hair and took a step back. Happy to have the twins do his dirty work.

"Here little kitty," called Sara, slowly circling.

Amy held her ground, eyes jumping between the identical girls.

Suddenly Amy had an idea. Maybe she was a nervous animal that might dart away. She glanced back at the goats. Sebastián and the twins had no interest in them. They were here for her. Õogly knew this, which is why she nodded at Amy, telling her to run.

61

WHOOSH!

Like a bolting horse, Amy was off! She darted under Sara's arms, narrowly making it, then charged down the hill.

"What!?" snapped Sebastián.

It took a few moments for Sarah and Sara to realise what had just happened.

"How - " stuttered Sarah, staring at the direction Amy had run.

"Go after her!" Sebastián grabbed the back of the girl's hoodies and pushed them forward. "If the cheerleading team see her covered in mud, they'll think I'm like *her*! I'll never make Captain!"

"But… but," stuttered Sara, still trying to work out how Amy had run under her arm.

"JUST GO!"

He looked like he was about to cry in frustration.

The twins turned to chase Amy. In the few seconds Amy had been running, she was almost out of sight. She was on all fours, thrusting her legs and arms forward as she galloped down a hill.

"Over there!" shouted Sarah, pointing down the hill.

Amy knew she had to reach the school gates to be safe. She'd no longer be out of bounds *and* the twins couldn't hurt her in front of the teachers. She was in luck, the gates were in sight. She glanced over her shoulder to check on the twins – they were right behind her!

"I can smell you!" shouted Sarah, reaching out to grab Amy's waist.

Amy's thumping heart hurt as she pushed harder.

Over the last few days she'd only eaten a goat diet of grass, hay and Custard Creams, so had very little energy. She looked back again and suddenly only one twin was behind her!

"Where's the other one!?" she panicked. Her eyes frantically searched the trees in front of her.

And then she spotted her.

Sara was standing at the school gates. She was blocking the only entrance, waiting for her.

Just as the twins had cheated in the cross-country race by finding a shortcut, they'd done the same thing here: cutting through the bushes to trap her from both ends. Amy had to think fast. She couldn't keep hurtling forward and she couldn't turn back.

What would Õogly do – what would Õogly do? She repeated in her head. An image flashed in her head: it was of Õogly jumping out of the circus ring.

Surely, Amy could do the same. Thanks to the herd, she knew these fields better than she knew how to ask for fresh hay in French ("*Est-ce que je peux avoir du foin frais?*") She saw an opening in the bushes, one that led to her house. Without a moment's hesitation, she took a swift left towards the main road.

Sarah stopped suddenly, narrowly avoiding skidding into a fence. "Go after her!" she shouted across the field to her sister.

Sara ran to meet her and looked down at where Amy had left. "And risk getting spotted in school uniform by an adult? You're bonkers! That's the road the teachers use to get to school. She won't have no chance of not getting caught."

Slowly, Sarah turned to stare at her sister in disbelief. "She won't have *no* chance of *not* getting caught," she repeated, stressing the words. "Your grammar is appalling. You've used a double negative and haven't even realised. How unattractive."

"Is this relevant, Sarah?! Amy's got away. What are we going to say to Sebastián?"

"Well, I'm *making* it relevant as I feel it more important than some freak out-running us."

Even in desperate times like this the identical girls didn't let their standards drop. Amy had beaten them in every test so things between the sisters were a tad tense.

"What are we going to say to beautiful Sebastián?" Sara asked again, pointing towards the road, Amy in the distance.

"You're not going to say anything, you can barely string a sentence together without hurting yourself."

Sara took a step back. "Fine by me. You can deliver the bad news while I stand looking pretty."

"Pfffft, you? Pretty?" her cruel sister teased. "*You're* the most hideous one in the family."

"Well you look identical to me so if I'm hideous, so are you."

She had her there.

Meanwhile, all the time the twins were throwing insults back at each other, clever Amy had escaped. She was now in sight of her home. She ran along the pavement, ignoring the turning heads of a couple of neighbours, then darted down the driveway, into the house, and up the stairs to her bedroom.

"Phewwwwwwwwww," she exhaled loudly, heart still pumping. She bent forward, ready to collapse on the floor in relief but found she couldn't. There was so much excitement and fear running through her body. She paced around her room, stepping over clumps of mud and thinking about what had just happened; Sebastián knew about the Goat Kingdom, she almost got expelled and she'd outrun the twins. It was all too much for one afternoon. Finally, she felt her legs give up, turning to jelly beneath her. She fell back onto her unmade bed.

"Ouch! What's this?" Something sharp jabbed her bare arms.

She rolled over and heard a creasing sound. She sat on a squashed piece of paper. More than that, it was an envelope, with her name on it.

Being only 10, Amy rarely received post, so

this was very exciting. She was looking forward to being an adult when she'd get loads of post. Be it bills or a letter to say she was being kicked out of her home, she didn't care as long as it came in the post.

She sat up, studying the envelope. It had mud and grass stuck to it. It had also been nibbled in the corner. Excitedly, she ripped it open with her teeth and pulled out a homemade card. She opened the card and read:

To Amy,

I have seen you at the Goat Kingdom and would love to become friends! Please meet me tomorrow at 10:00am at Godstone Farm, next to the donkey pen.

From a fellow goat, Billy. X

p.s. meeeeeeeeeeh!

Amy dropped the card, letting it fall to the ground. She couldn't believe what she had read. A fellow goat had noticed *her* at the pen and wanted to become friends! Another goat friend! Then her, Õogly and this new goat called Billy, could become a group of three. That's enough to start her own goat band. What would be their name!? She'd have to fight Õogly for lead singer.

Suddenly the house shook as the front door slammed shut.

"Amy? Sebastián?" called her mum. "Is someone home?" The was a suspicious tone in her voice like she wanted to catch someone misbehaving. Then came a long pause. "What's all this mud in the hallway?"

In a panic, Amy grabbed the card from the floor and dashed to her wardrobe. She opened the doors and climbed inside, moving a pile of muddy trainers out of the way. She closed the doors behind her, plummeting into darkness. Then, she held her breath.

"Amy, are you in here?" called Mum, walking into her room without knocking.

Amy watched through the thin slit between the wardrobe doors as her Mum inspected her room. She stopped at a piece of fresh mud. For a second Amy thought she was going to bend down and sniff it to track how fresh it was, but luckily, she turned on her heels and left.

"Phewwww," sighed Amy, taking a huge gulp of air. She leaned against the back of the wardrobe, soft clothes smelling of washing powder hung around her. She had to sit in the wardrobe for a long two hours until it was the correct time to be home from school. This didn't bother her. With the thin slit of light between the doors she re-read her card over and over. She kept imagining her new goat band with Õogly on drums. The excitement was just too much.

Amy decided there and then, if tomorrow went well, she'd dedicate her life to being a goat.

9
To meet a goat

Amy glanced down at her watch. It was almost 10:00am. In her hands, she grasped a thin paper bag of seeds and food pellets. She'd picked the bag up at Godstone Farm shop, where she was meeting Billy, her new goat friend. As she walked, she happily dipped into the bag. She enjoyed the browny-green pellets most. Dry, old grass that soaked up the moisture in her mouth. Long after swallowing, her tongue would find clumps caught in her gums like stuck Haribo.

"Almost there," Amy said to herself, pulling up her hood to keep the rain off.

Before going to bed last night Amy was so excited about coming as a goat today. It made her so happy that she could barely sleep! But as the night stretched on and she lay there awake in the empty room, she started to doubt herself. Her mind kept replaying how horrid Sebastián and the twins had been yesterday when chasing her. By morning she'd lost all her confidence. And so, she'd come as a human so walking like a human, as opposed to being on her hands and knees like a goat.

"Any minute now," Amy said quietly to herself, leaning against the donkey pen. She tried to look relaxed even though her tummy was spinning like a washing machine. She didn't mind the wait at first as it helped her nerves. But after 30 minutes of waiting, her nerves turn to irritation.

"This isn't a great impression to make when

69

meeting a new friend," she said, eyes searching the farm. They landed on a plump goat waddling towards her. Its hooves crunched along the gravel path.

"You're here!" She waved frantically.

The goat stopped in its tracks, staring blankly at the girl.

"How are you?!" she shouted, feeling very excited as the animal looked like they'd be a good dancer, perfect for her idea of starting a goat band with this third member.

The goat glanced over its shoulder to see if she was speaking to someone else. Suddenly Amy spotted the goat's bulging udders below its belly. She was meant to be meeting a male goat, Billy.

"*Oh*, you're not what, I mean *who*, I thought," she said, embarrassed. Being new to the goat world, Amy often got the gender of the animals mixed up. The goat carried on its way, slightly offended.

A few moments later Amy spotted an even cooler goat. She quickly took her hood down and combed her fringe through her fingers.

"Ah, this must be you!"

However, this handsome goat scurried straight past. It didn't even look her way. Amy remembered her mother saying how attractive men have a habit of doing that.

Very soon the seconds ticked to minutes then rolled to an hour. With soggy socks and shoes, Amy's knees started knocking together in the cold. Despite being soaked through, her throat was very dry. The way it goes just before you cry.

"He's not coming," she said sadly. Tears started

to fall. "Why did I let myself think he would come?"

All at once, Amy's ears picked up a noise. It sounded like a person laughing. She wiped the tears away and swung round to see where it came from.

CACKLE CACKLE CACKLE!

It went again. It was getting louder. Closer. The more she listened, the more she recognised it. It was bringing back a memory. A very recent memory.

"I know that noise," she said. She could feel her heart sinking but couldn't work out why. "I heard it yesterday. Yes! Yesterday! I was in the Goat Kingdom and standing behind me was…"

"She fell for it! I can't believe she fell for it!"

Amy's stomach dropped. Slowly she turned on her heels, her body tight, preparing for the person she would see. Or rather, the *persons* she would see.

"Clever Sebastián" shouted Sarah, skipping towards her, howling with laughter. "This was all his idea. He insisted, no, *begged* us to believe you'd fall for it."

"Yeah, imagine that," said Sara, taking over. "We were all like 'Amy-Wamey is stupid, but she's not *so* stupid to think a goat would want to be her friend. But he was right, you really are that stupid!"

"He's right about so many things, I just love him," said Sarah, slightly off-topic.

Amy didn't know how to respond. She looked past the twins, keeping an eye out for Billy, her new goat friend.

"Oh my," said Sarah, covering her mouth in disbelief. "She still doesn't get it, does she? It's a set-up!" she shouted, waving her arms in front of Amy like she was blind. "There is no Billy goat, you idiot!

71

We made him up!"

Amy slowly realised what was happening. At once she wanted the ground to swallow her up. To disappear. Forever.

"Finally, she gets it," continued Sarah, clapping slowly.

"I know, Sara. And look at her *coat*. It's like something our big sister would throw up after drinking too much beer."

"Oh wait, wait, look how wet her hair is. She's been standing in the rain acting desperate, waiting for her goat Prince to turn up. A rabbit boyfriend would be better with her giant rabbit teeth."

The sisters were talking *about* Amy *in front* of Amy like she didn't exist. It was an utterly unkind thing to do. Especially to someone whose dreams had just come crashing down.

"But I don't understand…" Amy said, finally speaking. "Why…" But then she stopped.

Just past the bullies, Amy saw something else. More people were coming towards her. Her classmates. The classmates she barely knew, who made no effort to be her friend. They were all pointing and laughing. Amy felt like she was now standing at the front of the assembly with everyone staring at her. All 200 of them.

Sarah walked up behind Amy and whispered into her ear. "After our little run-in yesterday we felt it our duty to warn the rest of the school that there's a goat freak among us." Amy could feel the bully's hot breath as she spoke. "A goat-freak that likes to be *friends* with goats and likes to *smell* like goats and likes to roll around in *poo* with goats."

"And you know what they said, Sis?"

"What's that?" replied Sis. "After we kindly warned our loyal school friends, who may I remind, we've been at school with *way* longer than you," Sara turned and glared at her classmates "… they said we were liars!"

"Us, liars!?"

"Yeah, I know Sis, it's despicable, isn't it?"

Now the whole class was watching. Some shook their heads embarrassed, not wanting to gawk at Amy standing alone. While others smirked, laughing loudly with the twins.

Sarah or Sara continued, "Your brother had the idea of *showing* the rest of the school that we were telling the truth. He wrote that pathetic card and left it in your room. All we had to do was invite the school to show them how desperate the new girl is to be friends with a goat."

"I'm not desperate!!!" screamed Amy, suddenly shocked at her outburst.

So were the twins, who shared a nervous look, but carried on.

"Well, who knows what would have happened had a goat shown up today? You'd probably let a goat give you a make-over, cut your ugly hair and do your make up."

"That would be an improvement," piped in Sara.

Things were getting out of hand. Amy could stand there all day defending herself, but she knew no one would listen to her. The bullies would twist her words just like an irritating sibling does when they wind you up so tightly all you want to do is smack them round the head… hard.

Amy knew better than to reply to the girls. Although, this wasn't her reason for keeping quiet.

73

As the girls spoke, she listened. And well, there was a lot of truth in what they were saying. Amy *did* like to be friends with goats, eat hay and roll around in poo. Well, maybe not the poo bit, yet. If the chance occurred then yes, Amy would LOVE for a goat to give her a make-over. From what she'd seen at the Goat Kingdom, they were really trendy.

Amy looked down at the paper bag of animal feed she'd been clutching in fear. She released her grip and saw she'd eaten most of the pellets, along with the paper bag. She wasn't ashamed. She thought back to this morning. Before leaving and she'd gone to the toilet in Colin's vegetable patch, right next to the sprouting carrots, just as a goat would do. Once again, she wasn't ashamed.

"You're right," said Amy, looking up. She locked eyes with the twins.

The bullies stopped sniggering. "Huh?"

"I said, you're right. Everything you've said is true. I like goats more than humans, especially you two *slugs*. And I enjoy climbing on bales of hay and then eating the hay, *especially* when it's muddy. And I chew all kinds of things from paper bags and curtains to textbooks and smelly pants." She paused and looked in the crowd. She was trying to spot someone. "Jenny, it was me who ate your pencil case last Tuesday in History class."

A scrawny girl gave a big huff.

"But you know what, I don't care. Well, I'm sorry about your pencil case Jenny, I'll ask my stepdad about buying you a new one. But the point I'm trying to make is, it's great being a goat!"

Now Amy stepped forward and spoke to everyone.

"You can eat food off the floor and sleep outside. You don't have to brush your teeth, wash your hair, or your feet or face! I'm free to be myself, for the first time in my life. I finally feel happy as me. You should all try it!"

Sarah and Sara watched the girl as their mouths hung open. It was like she was giving a thank you speech at the Oscars. They weren't expecting this. They thought she'd cry and run home like yesterday.

Sarah scowled. "Shut up, you silly -"

But she was unable to finish her sentence for what happened next.

Amy opened her mouth wide, took a gigantic breath in, and exploded with:

"Mehhhhhhhhhhhhhhh!"

Everyone froze.

The twins gawked at Amy, horrified at the goat noise. It certainly served its purpose of drowning out the bully because when Sarah opened her mouth to speak again, she got no further.

"Shut up, you -"

"*Mehhhhhhhhhhhhhhh,*" cried Amy again, this time louder so the sound travelled out of the farm "*Mehhhhhhhhhhhhhhhh! Mehhhhhhhhhhhhhhhh! Mehhhhhhhhhhhhhhhh!*" she bleated so perfectly that her classmates thought she was transforming into a goat before their very eyes. Should they help her? But how? Call a doctor... or a vet?

Amy laughed loudly. The kind of laugh that made her belly jump up and down uncontrollably. Full of confidence, she leapt onto a soggy bale of hay. Now all her classmates could see her. She took a deep breath in to make the same noise. But was beaten to it.

"*Mehhhhhhhhhhhhhhhh.*"

Everyone froze for the second time that day. Even Amy. She looked round to see where the noise came from.

Then silence. Everything had fallen quiet.

The whistling of the wind stopped. Even the shuffle of gravel fell silent. Suddenly Amy felt the bale of hay moving beneath her. It was ever so slightly twisting back and forth, making her wobble. She looked down at the twins and saw the stones by their trainers moving. Tiny bits of gravel were trembling like bubbling water in a boiling pan.

"What's happening!?" screamed Sara as the ground began to shake. "What the hell have you done? You freak!"

And then, Amy saw it. Across the farm at the very tip of the hill.

Goats.

10 of them, no, 20 of them, no, BILLIONS of them. Hurtling down the hill, straight at them. They galloped like a stampede of wild animals. The ground shook like an earthquake.

If the goats didn't stop, they'd run straight into them. Amy's throat turned dry.

This was exactly what they were planning to do.

10
The transformation

Goats gushed down the hill, flooding the farm
like a river bursting its banks. Mess and chaos
followed in every direction they ran. Animal pens
were smashed open, sending shards of wood soaring.
Flower beds were ripped apart, sending bulbs flying
like rubble in a shell explosion.

Amy watched from the safety of her hay bale.
Everyone was screaming, making a quick dash out of
the way. Those that didn't run held on to others for
support. Small classmates clung to chubby arms. But
it was useless, soon everyone was being chased by a
goat.

Amy saw a Golden Guernsey goat (most common in England) bite a classmate's ponytail and then chew at her shoelaces after she fell. The white fleecy Angora goats (commonly confused with sheep) were tormenting a scared boy named Amara. He'd dropped his coat and in one gulp an Angora ate it. Even Jenny, the girl with the eaten pencil case, became a victim. A group of blonde Cashmere goats chased her in circles around the farm shop. That poor girl, first her pencil case eaten by a classmate, and now she was being chased by manic farm animals.

Sara, the bully stood in the centre of the mess.

"What is going on here!?" she screamed. "You told them to do this!" She pointed up at Amy with a fierce stare.

Before Amy could answer, a curious short-haired Nubian goat (known to have very large, droopy udders) kicked Sara in the rear and then sat on her face. Sarah, her identical twin sister saw this and silently slipped away.

Sara's words stuck with Amy. Had she caused this? But how? She couldn't help but notice how none of the goats were attacking her. She also couldn't help but notice the tight feeling in her stomach: excitement.

She stared back to the hill the goats had come from. There was a single goat still standing there. Amy squinted, trying to make out the animal's markings. Then she spotted it. Completely black fur but for the white line from its hoof, up its knobbly leg and over its back,

Õogly.

"She did this," Amy said, slowly realising.

79

Õogly had heard Amy bleating and thought it was a call for help. Quickly she'd rounded up the goat herd and charged down the hill into the farm. And the result was this: a very peculiar war between goat and human. As far as wars go it was rather tame. But as time went on, it grew to more than just goats.

The larger mountain goats with strong curly horns had smashed into the animal pens. Fences were ripped from the soil, allowing pigs, cows and gees to run free. Even the donkey pen Amy had waited at was now open. Ethel the donkey hadn't stepped outside her pen for 17 long years and now she was eating a lost shoe.

From the hay bale, Amy looked round and smiled, recognising the people being chased and bitten. Among the mess were some of her teachers and members of her mother's Circus Society.

"Take cover!" shouted a very hair man. Amy recognised it as Norman the local milkman and Circus Society member. He was cowering under an overturned food trough being splatted with brown sheep food. Every time a llama charged past, he quivered.

"Hold on tight, me kiddies!" came another cry from the familiar voice of Mr McSporran, Amy's form teacher. Mr McSporran had been in the adventure playground with his two sons when the charge took place. Now they were clinging onto the monkey bars, holding themselves up off the ground. Naughty chickens jumped up trying to peck them.

"I can't hold on Daddy, my arms are achy," little Jimmy whined, as he slowly started to sink.

Amy was loving it. As she stood taking it all in,

ducking from the odd low-flying duck, she had an almighty urge to be involved. Not to be involved as you might think a sweet young child ought to be involved (apologising to the farmer and helping the elderly escape). No, to be involved by adding to the destruction.

Then it suddenly happened. Amy felt something bubbling inside her. It was bubbling in her toes and her ankles and up the back of her legs. It was shooting down her arms and bouncing in her belly, making her excited.

"This is it," she said. "It's happening!"

Suddenly, she erupted like a fizzy drink exploding from a can.

"Mehhhhhhhhhhhhhhhhhhhhhhhhhhhhhhhhhhhhhhhhhhh!"

Amy cried like a goat. And what a cry it was! It bellowed through the farm louder than a giant's belch. It shook every chicken and child with its ear-splitting sound. How could such a superb-sounding goat noise come from this small girl?

She wiped the dribble from her mouth. Her heart pounded. She looked up and was shocked to notice everyone had stopped. Every child, llama, chicken and pig stood, looking up at her.

A little girl with braids tugged at her daddy's sleeve and whispered. "What's going to happen next, Daddy?"

But Amy left no time for an answer. She ripped out her rainbow hair ribbon, letting her dirty hair fall free. She grabbed her trainers and threw them into a water trough. Now she was down onto all fours, just like a farm animal.

"She's becoming a goat!" an onlooker cried.

At this point, the crowd went berserk! They reacted as if nuclear war had just been announced! Women were screaming, babies were screaming, and even Ethel the donkey was screaming.

Amy leapt down from the bale of hay, landing in a suspiciously smelly pile of mud. She bounded over to join the herd.

"*Bonjour, bonjour!*" said the goats, rearing their horns with Amy's flat head. The herd was so proud of Amy. She was choosing to become a goat. They knew she could never grow horns and hooves like them, but it didn't matter. She was choosing happiness, and that meant acting like a goat.

They surrounded her, licking her face with their long rough tongues. If Amy didn't smell like a goat before, she certainly did now. But Amy was too excited to simply stand around being licked. And unlike sheep, goats rarely spend all day simply standing in one spot.

Amy longed to try out her new freedom. And she knew exactly where to start. She bounced out of the farm, leaving her trail of destruction behind her. She bounced over fields and fences. Sometimes she stopped to sniff and eat a crunchy leaf. Her hands and knees were thick with heavy mud as they worked as hooves. Soon she reached the road where she lived. She felt it was about time she told her parents the truth. Over the last week her mother had grown wearily suspicious and Colin wearily wheezy. As Amy neared her home, she heard a roar of sneezes from her stepdad.

"*Achhhooooooo! Achhhooooooo!*"

"Poor Colin must be able to smell me getting

close," said Amy as she trotted proudly up her driveway on all fours.

"*Achhhoooooo!*"

The sneezes exploded through the front door making it rattle.

"Won't you get yourself a hanky!" Amy's mother cried from inside the house.

Outside on the porch, Amy pressed her nose against the doorbell. Bells played out through the house.

"There's someone at the door - *achhhoooooo!*" shouted Colin.

"Yes, I know there's someone at the door," Mum snapped. "I'm surprised you can hear the bell with all the racket you're making! And you still haven't got yourself a hanky."

Amy's mother swung open the front door with a fixed smile. "I can only apologise for the delay, something in the air seems to be troubling my partner's nose."

She stopped talking.

She looked down.

"*Mehhhhhhhh!*"

Amy charged into the house, through her mother's legs, sending her falling to her bottom.

"What on *earth* are you doing, Amy!?"

Amy stampeded into her parents' peaceful Sunday afternoon like a bull in a china shop. No, like a goat in a tidy Kent living room. She raced across the white cashmere carpet, leaving a trail of muddy hand prints. Then she bit into the flowery curtains, ripping the whole rail down.

"What has got into you, Amy!?" shouted Mum,

still sat on the floor in the hallway. But Amy wasn't listening to Mum. Instead, she was heading straight to the Egyptian cotton rug she'd been craving to chew for weeks. Amy leapt over it, sinking her buck teeth into it. Dribble ran down her chin.

"Oh no you don't, you pesky girl!" her mother shouted, jumping onto her daughter. She desperately pulled at Amy's legs, but with no success, so searched the living room for a new idea.

Suddenly she spotted a copy of the *Daily Express*, and rolled it into a long tube. She turned back to her daughter and started swatting her around the head like she was an irritating mosquito.

"Let. It. Go. Let. It. Go. Drop. It. This. Minute!"

Colin, who had momentarily stepped out to get a hanky, now returned to an utter circus. "I hadn't finished reading that paper!" he announced over the chaos. "And that's your daughter you're bonking on the head."

"No daughter of mine would be chewing the expensive Egyptian cotton rug!"

Amy's stepdad looked down at the wrestling pair. "Don't, Amy. That rug was a gift." He explained this in a very matter-of-fact kind of way. He appeared oblivious that his stepdaughter had rejected her human life to become a goat. Amy's mother, however, had certainly noticed.

"So this is what's got into you, hmm? You've chosen this life of a *'goat'*," she huffed while tugging at her daughter's back legs, desperate to save the rug. "We should have listened to Sebastián who told us *weeks* ago. And then we *really* should have clocked when we found those 'How To Be A Goat' magazines in your room!"

Out of nowhere, Amy lost interest in the rug and charged up the stairs to her bedroom. Her parents raced after her. Mum shoved poor Colin out of the way as he fumbled around, continually sneezing.

Once in her bedroom, Amy ripped her pillows apart with her big teeth. Feathers fluttered around the room and out onto the hallway.

"Oh no, feathers make me sneeze terribly, *achhhoooooo!*" Colin sneezed, falling back down the staircase.

Now that Amy was a goat, she didn't want to sleep in a normal, boring, human bed. She wanted to make herself a goat pen.

"You better be prepared to tidy up after yourself Amy," said Mum, standing in the bedroom doorway. "It's fine to redecorate your room on occasion, but I won't have you turning it into a pigsty just because you feel like it one day."

"It's not a pigsty, dear," sniffed Colin, climbing to the top step on his hands and knees. "It's a pen for a goat."

"I don't care what you call it! Enough is enough Amy. I've been incredibly patient during this 'experimental' stage of your life. I've turned a blind eye to you chewing the tea towels and that collection of hay in the corner of the bathroom. But this must stop now. And preferably before I take you to your stamp collecting class tomorrow morning."

"I think that might need to be missed," said Colin who was sitting on the landing, gasping for air.

Mother remained in the doorway, feathers fluttering around her. She watched her daughter, silently panicking at how to put a stop to this.

11
The morning after the night before

"Won't you count me in, Norman? From the start, please."

"The very, *very* start?"

"Yes, the very, *very* start. Hold on, move that chopping board. It can slide into the racks behind you."

"Done. Ready?"

"Oh, and that saucepan. Into the bottom drawer, please."

"Okay."

"I just need to push myself up onto my head. Nearly there… oh… yes, I'm up. Start the track!"

Norman the local milkman and Amy's mother were practising her circus routine in the kitchen. It was just four days until opening night and Mum was desperately trying to perfect the art of doing a headstand whilst balancing on the hump of a camel. (See Diagram B).

"Excellent my dear, you are up balancing on your head quite poetically," said Norman. "Now don't forget to smile." He pulled his mouth wide, acting like a school photographer desperate to get a miserable child to grin, "Shall I bring in Yasmin?"

"Bring in whom?" enquired Mum, looking at the world upside down. She was doing a headstand in the middle of the large kitchen table. Her face was turning the colour of a very ripe tomato. All of her body was balancing on a folded tea towel.

Diagram B

Skills required:
• Balancing on the top of the pointy hump of a camel while it's dancing
• Keeping balance should the animal spit
• Smiling and looking totally at ease to the paying audience

"Yasmin," repeated Norman. "I brought her with me, she's tied up outside in the garden." Norman pushed open the backdoor to reveal a humongous golden camel standing in the doorway. The camel was bigger than the back door so all Mum could see were four very long, very scrawny hairy legs. They were golden in colour with sharp, pointy knees. The whiff of wet camel flew up Mum's nose. She could hear the faint sound of its wet sloppy mouth chewing its own saliva.

"In you come, girl," called Norman, leading Yasmin into the kitchen with a red collar. "Careful with your head there, don't knock the ceiling lights."

"Norman, has the blood rushed to my head making me imagine things or have you brought a giant camel into my nice, clean kitchen?"

"Achoooooooo!" sneezed Colin from his study upstairs.

"That answers it. If Colin is sneezing, there is certainly a camel in the house *and* it's licking the draining board."

Norman swivelled round to see Yasmin's long, pink tongue licking the coffee mugs.

Using the back of his hand, Norman swiftly knocked the mugs into the sink of water, as if nothing had happened.

"Right," he said, tugging at Yasmin's collar to get her head away from the sink. "This time you'll have to climb onto dear Yasmin's back and then get into the headstand position. She's very well-behaved."

Then there was a crash as a mug fell and smashed on the hard tiled floor.

Norman's head snapped up at Yasmin. "Where did you get that mug from? You naughty girl!"

The camel ignored the man, eyes rolled over, mouth slowly chewing.

"She's *usually* very well-behaved," he continued. "Except she does have a bad habit of escaping from her pen at the circus. I don't know how she does it."

"That's all very well Norman," said Mum, "but I don't feel I'll have time to go up on Yasmin today." She carefully lowered herself off her head so that the world was the right way up again. The camel looked even larger from this angle.

"I must wake up Amy for stamp-collecting class which starts in 23 minutes." Climbing down from the table, she warily slid behind the huge animal to reach the other side of the kitchen. The kitchen wasn't particularly small but adding a camel doesn't leave much room for anything else. She held her breath as she neared its pooey bottom.

Norman stared at the woman in utter shock. "Firstly, our show is just FOUR DAYS AWAY! And secondly, you're allowing Amy to go to her stamp-collecting class following that stunt she pulled at Godstone Farm yesterday?" Norman buried his head into Yasmin's long neck and whimpered. "I woke up in a sweat in the night having terrible night horrors of an over-friendly dwarf goat biting my bottom!"

Amy's Mum knew Norman was right, she just refused to accept any of it. She had received a wave of phone calls from horrified parents and members of the Circus Society who'd been at the farm during yesterday's 'incident'. Instead of sitting Amy down to have a stern conversation, she'd decided the most suitable step forward was to totally ignore *everything* and *anything* goat related. She chose not to hear the phone constantly ringing with calls from appalled parents. She chose not to smell the mud in the house *and* she chose not to see her daughter leaving her dinner to instead eat piles of limp grass. Amy's mum would continue to treat Amy like a human and that was that.

"Yes, she will be very late for her stamp-collecting class if I don't get her up soon," recited Mum, like a robot, staring straight ahead.

Looking flummoxed, Norman stared up at the camel, then back at Mum. "But goats don't collect stamps."

"Amy!" screamed Mum, pushing past Norman, slightly elbowing him in the face. "You better be up and dressed for stamp-collecting class!"

Meanwhile, upstairs in Amy's bedroom, she was having the most marvellous dream. She was dreaming she'd started a stampede with a herd of goats. They'd trampled Sarah and Sara, the identical twins with almost identical names. And she was dreaming she'd chosen to become a goat, causing mayhem at home. *And*, rather unrelated, she was dreaming there was a camel in the kitchen and her mother was shouting at her to get out of bed.

"Amy, are you listening to me? We are leaving in 10 minutes!"

Amy jumped awake. She saw the mud and feathers covering the carpet. Everything she dreamt was true. She went to kick off her blanket then realised she wasn't under one. She wasn't even in her bed. She'd been sleeping curled up in the corner of her bedroom, under the window, in a little basket of hay and wood chippings.

"I'm coming up there, Amy. You'd better be dressed," shouted Mum, stomping up the stairs to her daughter's bedroom. Without warning, she swung open the bedroom door to find her daughter lying among hay on the recently vacuumed carpet. She gave a horrified cry. *"Ahhhhhhhhh!* You're not even up, Amy! I said we're leaving in 10 minutes."

Despite the look of terror on Mum's face, she refused to acknowledge the goatly sight she saw. So, ever so calmly she said, "Your book of collected stamps is in the hallway, should you be looking for it."

"Mehhhhhhh," replied Amy, like a goat.

Her mother jumped like she'd been touched by a ghost. "Ahh! You frightened me, Amy. What a peculiar and out-of-character noise to come from a smart child who is, might I stress, a h-u-m-a-n. I'll be waiting for you in the car." She turned to leave then paused. She turned back and spoke into the bedroom, not looking at Amy on the floor. "Watch out for the camel as you come down."

And with that, her mother slammed the bedroom door shut and stomped back downstairs.

"Get that camel away from the fruit bowl!"

Amy relaxed back into the wood chippings. She had no intention of going to her stamp-collecting class. It was another one of the activities her mother forced her to do to keep her unhappy. It involved going to a stale, smelly church hall to sit at a sticky table talking about stamps. Amy found this very dull and often had the destructive desire to eat everyone's stamps. Especially the rare, expensive ones.

Instead, she'd already set herself a jam-packed

goat day. The plan was to get up, not wash, go meet Oogly and the herd, trot around and chew some plants for nine hours, return home, not wash, then go to bed. Tonight, she'd sleep in the garden and at dinner she'd demand all food be thrown on the ground, where she'd prefer to eat it.

Amy smiled to herself and had a big stretch. Then she clambered up onto all fours, like a goat. For her morning shower, she licked her hands and arms clean of grass stains. Unfortunately, her tongue didn't reach any other parts of her body, so they stayed dirty. Once done, she clambered onto a chair and stared at her reflection in the wardrobe mirror.

"I look a state," she said to herself. She stared at her muddy face wondering how she had managed to get mud above her eyebrow. Her thick brown hair was piled upon her head like a deserted bird's nest. If you tried to put a comb through it, it would snap.

"Perfect," she said smiling, having done nothing to tidy herself up.

"I'm waiting in the car!" cried Amy's mum from outside, sat in the driver's seat, gripping the wheel. "If you don't get down here in 2 seconds, I'll – umm – I'll give you the worst punishment of your life!"

Then, with absolutely no fear, Amy trotted out of her bedroom, down the stairs and past Mum, alone.

12
Into the woods

When Amy was with the goat herd, she was home. For her, being home wasn't a place, it was a feeling. With the goats, she could be anything. And nothing had to make sense. Last week Amy and Õogly sat speaking in French while eating German sausages. The next day a bunch of them rolled around in the mud and then tried on expensive perfumes to mask the smell. All the while without Mrs Moopleton the headmistress painting her grey or her mother's disapproving stare.

Today, like most days, Amy was most looking forward to seeing Õogly. She wanted to thank her for yesterday. If it wasn't for her rounding up the herd and storming the farm, Amy would still be acting like a human. Right now, she'd be sitting feeling miserable, being driven to her miserable stamp-collecting class, to do something miserable. How miserable.

Amy shuddered at the thought. She pushed her way head-first through the thistle bushes to reach the Goat Kingdom. The sound of happy goat cries and grime music filled her ears. She trotted over to her and Õogly's favourite hay bale, curled up like a cat, and waited.

"*Bonjour!*" Amy greeted a passing mountain goat she recognised from last week's Conga line. "*Où est Õogly?*" (Where is Õogly?)

The goat shrugged at the girl, not knowing Õogly's whereabouts. Amy couldn't help but feel the goat was embarrassed about the Conga line.

"Okay, I'll stay put!" she called after the animal.

Since meeting three weeks ago, Õogly and Amy had become inseparable. They were like two chocolate sticks of a KitKat, always side by side. For Amy; Õogly was the breath of fresh air that showed her what life could be. And for Õogly; Amy was like a little sister, someone exploding with questions who would, on occasion, give her beard a brush. It's fair to say they were the happiest of friends. They were best friends.

Amy stared up at the sky. It was sunny now, but an angry black cloud was heading their way. Growing impatient, she spotted two black baby kid goats with muddy hooves.

"Excuse me," she said, waving to get their attention. "Have you seen Õogly today?"

They looked at each other with big, green eyes and long lashes. They shook their heads.

"How odd, she's always here to meet me."

Amy pulled herself up and stood on tiptoes to get a better view of the Kingdom. Everyone was acting normal, taking advantage of the last of the day's sun. A large white Cashmere goat was blowing up a paddling pool. The smaller goats were jumping around excitedly in their bathing costumes. This wasn't anything Amy hadn't seen before. Her nerves were calmed slightly.

She decided to call out Õogly's name. Maybe she was had headphones on.

"Õogly!" she cried, cupping her mouth like a megaphone.

No one answered.

"I want to thank you for yesterday! Where are

you?"

Amy couldn't hear anything. The kid goats in the paddling pool were splashing around loudly. She noticed her palms had become sweaty.

"It's fine," she said, though not believing herself. "I'll just go and find you."

She trotted around the pen, sniffing the grass and trees, trying to pick up Õogly's scent. As she searched, she focused on her breathing. Slowly in then slowly out. She didn't want to panic. Yet. She started with the usual places; the trampoline, then this big smelly puddle they liked to jump in. But after 30 minutes of looking, Amy felt her stomach tighten. This wasn't normal behaviour. Something was wrong. She thought back to Sebastián. The last time she'd seen him was at this very pen. Standing proudly with the twins, terrifying the goats. Amy felt a wave of guilt remembering she'd left Õogly. She'd run away.

"If Sebastián and his cheerleading team have hurt her I..." she didn't want to finish the sentence.

Hearing the words, Amy could no longer control her nerves. She frantically galloped out of the pen towards the hilltop. The top of the hill was dangerous, no animals went there. Gales of wind roamed the hill like an angry monster. It would sweep up your feet, dragging you over the hill. The goats that did adventure up there, never returned.

Amy pictured this happening to Õogly. After all, when she sent the herd to Godstone Farm, she'd been standing at the top of this hill.

Running against the wind, Amy charged up the hill. The wind tugged at her hair, almost as a warning, pulling her back. Her eyes streamed with water, making it difficult to see how close to the edge she was. The black clouds arrived at the same time she did, turning everything dark. Behind her was the forest, now plummeted into the darkness like it was the middle of the night. Whenever Amy looked into a forest, she always felt there was someone hiding behind a tree, looking back.

"Õogly! Õogly!" she shouted across the open hilltop. The wind ravaged her feeble cry. She spun around frantically shouting again and again. She tripped over her feet, stumbling down the hill. Landing in a flat patch of grass she collapsed in tears.

"She's gone. It's all my fault -" she wailed loudly. So distraught at the thought of her lost friend, she didn't realise how close she'd been to falling off the hill. She rolled onto her side, sobbing. Then, between tears, she saw something move. A small flicker of white in the distant forest. Pushing herself up, she wiped her wet eyes to see better.

In the forest was the white tip of an Anglo-Nubian goat tail. Amy was now an expert in goat breeds; you could put any goat tail in front of her and she'd tell you the breed, age, and even gender of that animal.

"Õogly!" she shouted, running into the forest, forgetting her fears.

She leapt over tree roots, running to her friend. When Amy reached her, she wanted to look away.

Tangled among the thick roots of a giant tree was Õogly. She was lying in a way Amy had never seen a goat lie. Her four legs were sprawled out around her, instead of being tucked neatly under her body. Her long neck and head were resting against the tree trunk, unable to stay up on its own.

"What happened?" asked Amy, slowly bending down to be close to her friend. "Has someone hurt you?" She took the animal's soft floppy ear in her hand. It was ice cold.

Slowly, Õogly opened her eyes at the girl's touch. The animal's large circular eyes were glazed over. She was awake but clearly didn't know what was happening.

"We never come to this part of the woods," said Amy, peering over her shoulder at the dark trees.

"You're freezing. I think you're terribly ill."

Amy started racking her brain, thinking about how she could help her friend. When Amy became ill, her stepdad Colin looked after her. Despite having no medical experience, he'd diagnose Amy and Sebastián with all kinds of tropical diseases. He had a huge dusty book all about tropical diseases one might catch if one lived in the jungle. If Amy was suffering from a simple headache he would flick through the book and say, "I'm afraid it's not a headache. You're actually suffering from Pedunculated-Elephantiasis." Then, instead of bringing her some vegetable soup, which is what she'd really want, he'd start disinfecting everything in the house so the disease didn't spread further.

Looking down at Õogly now, Amy felt confident diagnosing Õogly with the flu (not Trichosporon-giganteum, which is what Colin would say).

"Shortness of breath, low energy, high fever," said Amy, listing off the symptoms on her fingers. "Yep, you've got flu is all!" Feeling relieved, Amy allowed a little smile.

"What you need is rest in a comfy, warm bed. As well as vegetable soup. I could even make you grass soup, I'm sure it can't be too difficult." She looked around, remembering where they were. "One thing's certain, you can't stay here. It's about to rain, you could die from the cold and wet!"

Amy touched Õogly's forehead to feel her temperature. Even during this short time, the animal's body temperature started rising. She was now boiling, breaking out in a sweat all over her fur.

Amy slid her arms under her friends' weak body,

ready to pick her up. But then something stopped her. She didn't know what she was doing.

"Where would I hide you? How would I get you in the house?" she said under her breath. "Of course, I'd have to hide you from my mother. She doesn't fully support my goat life so isn't ready to have my goat friends around quite so soon." She hesitated. "And I'd definitely have to keep you away from Sebastián. If his cheerleading friends found out that there was now a goat living at home, they'd drop him from the team. Not that I care, but he might try and hurt you!" She stopped for a third time. "Oh, and we can't forget Colin. He's allergic to every animal. His nose would sniff you out before anyone finds you."

Amy slowly removed her arms from under her friend. She couldn't risk it. The smile faded from her face. Bringing Õogly into the house meant risking so much. Feeling small she glanced over her shoulder at the huge forest surrounding them. It was now raining and their patch under the tree wouldn't keep them dry much longer.

"I can't leave you. I don't want to leave you."

She sighed deeply. The image of her running away, leaving the goats to Sebastián and the twins kept creeping back. Then, she pulled her friend onto her back and started home.

13

There was no doubt in Amy's mind that she would get in severe trouble

There was no doubt in Amy's mind that she would get in severe trouble. The first hurdle, which would certainly get her in severe trouble, was getting Õogly inside her house. The journey was across the drive, around the garden, through the kitchen, up the stairs, over the landing and into her bedroom. All without being seen.

'*Use the back door!*' one might say, but Mum and Colin were blocking it having a heated discussion over a cup of tea. And they didn't look to be in any hurry. Also, to add to the mess, Õogly had suddenly developed terrible wind. '*BARP!*' her goat bottom kept whistling in Amy's face, causing her to pass out from the smell. Amy didn't want to risk being sniffed out so decided to wait. The pair hid in Colin's vegetable patch, about two meters from the back door, waiting for the right time to run in. Until then, she eavesdropped on their conversation. Quickly she realised they were talking about her. And it didn't sound good.

"Mrs Moopleton was very strict on the phone," said Mum, clutching her mug of tea with both hands. "If it weren't for Amy's wonderfully improved grades, especially in French, they would have expelled her weeks ago! They can't have a student eating the art supplies. They're expensive, for one thing." She paused and sipped her tea. "Mrs Moopleton was so angry and DISTRESSED on the phone."

"Mrs Moopleton?" asked Colin. "As in *Edna* Moopleton? Why I remember her from when we were at school together as kids! She was the best painter in my class and had dreams of being the next Picasso. That's until her parents put an end to it and forced her to do Extra-Complicated-Mathematics instead. She was never happy again after that."

Mum wasn't listening. "I think she was physically painting a small child grey while speaking to me."

"Sounds like her," agreed Colin, pulling up his trousers which had started to fall down again. "But what good would come from expelling the girl? Surely with her impressive grades, she's an asset to the school." He suddenly paused and sniffed the air. "I say, was that you?"

"Was *what* me?"

"I think you know..."

"Whatever are you talking about?" disputed Mum, as her nose crinkled at the tip.

"OH PONG! No, I'll have you know I did not create that smell and I would expect more of you than to assume your partner was capable of producing such a stench."

Amy looked down at the unwell (and very smelly) Õogly and giggled.

Mum continued. "If I could bring your attention back to the important matter of your stepdaughter's education. I'd like to assure you Mrs Moopleton and I reached an agreement." She stopped and placed her mug in the sink. "Amy has one chance... Should she step out of line once more with anything gazelle-like..."

"It's not gazelle, my dear. The girl has chosen to become a *goat*."

Mum's hands gripped the kitchen counter edge like she trying to stop herself from ripping it apart.

"As I was saying," she closed her eyes and breathed. "Amy has one chance. Every teacher, student and dinner lady will be watching her and waiting. There's even a reward for whoever catches her acting like a goat. And what a reward it is - unlimited tickets to Disney World *and* queue-jump *and* unlimited birthday cake, made by Mickey Mouse himself." She looked over her shoulder, checking no one was listening. "Once the time comes - and it will come as Amy can't stop acting...different, she will be expelled from St Andrews School of Controlled Excellence & Unoriginality. Then, she will be home-schooled by Mrs Moopleton until she is 30 years old. Classes will take place every day, including Christmas Day and will focus on the most boring subjects, like Extra-Complicated-Mathematics."

"NO!" squealed Amy loudly, forgetting where she was for a moment.

Colin glanced round into the garden and spotted the patch of cabbages shaking. "Did you see that?"

Mum glared at him. "Oh heavens, aren't you distracted today!" She threw up her arms in defeat.

"You're not listening to a word I'm saying!"

"Must be the new fertiliser."

Colin looked back at Mum who looked to be trying to kill him with a single stare.

"That's not true, I *am* listening," he said, steeling a quick look back at the cabbage. "Should we share this information with Amy?"

"Certainly not. I can't keep track of her at the best of times. She's meant to be at Stamp Collecting class right now. Heaven knows what the girl would be like should she know what's at risk."

Colin paused and scrunched up his forehead, thinking hard for a solution.

"We could get her some kind of lead? Like a dog. That would help us keep track of her."

Amy's mother took a deep breath in and erupted, "WILL YOU STOP SUGGESTING THINGS THAT RELATE TO MY DAUGHTER BEING AN... AN... ANIMAL!"

She slammed her hands on the draining board and marched out of the kitchen. Colin was rather taken aback by the reaction, so refilled her mug from the teapot and wandered after her. Luckily for Amy, this left the kitchen completely clear.

"Now's our chance," she said, dusting the mud from her knees. She took one step then stopped. She replayed Mum and Colin's conversation in her mind. Allowing Õogly into the house and being caught meant expulsion. That's an eternity with Mrs Moopleton – the person who wants to stop Amy's dreams coming true, just as hers had been. She couldn't let that happen. She looked down at Õogly lying among the thick cabbage leaves. Seeing her this weak made her so sad.

Only Amy could help her.

"Okay. But we cannot get caught."

Amy lifted Õogly's front hoof and shook it as if making a deal. Stepping over the beetroot sprouts, they snuck towards the back door. Amy led Õogly like she was drunk, falling all over the place, unable to keep her eyes open. The back door squeaked as it was pushed open. Staying close to the walls they slipped across the kitchen, (which still smelt strongly of camel) and then darted up the stairs. Mum and Colin were in the sitting room, now squabbling about the bite marks in the curtains. Once upstairs, Amy launched into her bedroom and slammed the door shut. Õogly collapsed onto the carpet, exhausted.

Over the next few hours, Amy tended to Õogly's every need. At first, it was simple: keeping the room nice and warm, plumping pillows while she slept in Amy's bed. She stroked Õogly's long ears and read popular goat literature such as *Three Billy Goats Gruff* and Michael Morporgo's *War Horse*. *War Horse* doesn't feature any goats but is still an exquisite book enjoyed by all. Things became more challenging when Õogly became hungry. As Amy turned the final page of *Animal Farm* she was interrupted by a low rumbly growl.

"Heavens! Was that your stomach!?" she asked Õogly.

Õogly pointed into her wide mouth with her hoof.

To settle the goat's rumbly stomach Amy said she'd make grass soup. But she'd deliberately delayed this by reading book after book. Making the soup meant leaving Õogly alone upstairs. This made her nervous. What if Colin walked in? What if Õogly walked out?

The goat's hairy pink stomach growled again, rippling up and down.

Amy stood by the bed. "You have to promise me you'll stay right here. My stepdad is just across the landing in the bathroom. He's treating Stewart the cat to a bubble bath with Mum's expensive bath soaps." Amy smelt the strawberry bubble bath drifting into her room. "I suspect you being here has brought on his allergies and he's blaming the cat. If you make any sound he'll come charging in and go utterly berserk."

"*Meeeeeehhh,*" cried Õogly weakly.

Amy nodded her head, accepting this as a yes. And with that she licked Õogly on the nose and scurried out of the room.

"Please don't make a sound," she whispered, closing the door softly behind her.

Amy couldn't help but feel it was all about to go very wrong.

14
Grass soup

On all fours like a true goat, Amy bounded down
the stairs and into the garden. Õogly was ill upstairs
in her bedroom so Amy was making her grass soup.
At once, the girl started chomping at the grass,
ripping up plants with her teeth and dropping them
into Colin's muddy gardening bucket. She focused on

all the weeds that goats love and gardeners hate. These were the dandelions, nettles and thistles. Any tough plants she could get her big teeth around she tore up and flung in the bucket with a plonk.

"There you are!" said Mum, sticking her head out the kitchen window making Amy jump. "What on earth has got into you *now*!? Are you after a snack? You look like you're hungry."

"*Meeeehhh*," bleated Amy, not looking up.

"I'll prepare you a ham sandwich at once. Humans like ham sandwiches." She slipped her head back inside.

With the bucket almost full of weeds, Amy gripped the swinging handle with her mouth and carried it into the kitchen. Sebastián was inside, sitting in front of the TV on his bean bag. It was the first time she'd seen him since he'd tricked her with the fake goat card. Amy's stomach winced with nerves when she saw him.

"That terrible smell's come back, Mum," he announced to the room, not looking up.

Mum was raiding the bread bin. "Quiet now, My Little Hero. Amy has simply been playing in the garden. She's found a new interest in gardening which explains why she's carrying Colin's gardening bucket with her...urm...mouth." She hesitated momentarily, looking at the trail of dirt her daughter was leaving. She forced herself to continue. "Yes, it's gardening. Amy, we have a lovely gardening book that lists all the Latin names of plants, wouldn't you like to read that instead of eating mud?"

Amy took no notice. She was busy shoving

clumps of grass into a large bowl with water.

"Oh, I am mistaken," corrected Mum, watching her daughter rattle through the pots and pans. "It seems your sister is actually interested in cooking. You like cooking Sebastián, why don't the two of you bake your mother a delicious Victoria sponge cake."

Sebastián put his headphones in and slouched further into the bean bag.

Amy was far too busy to be upset by her brother today. She wanted to make the best grass soup possible. In a large casserole pan she dropped the muddy dandelions, nettles and thistles, making sure not to clean them first. Then she poured 750ml of water, added salt and pepper to season, and finished with a big stir with a wooden spoon. It filled the kitchen with the smell of muddy, warm Wellington boots.

Suddenly, a large crash came from upstairs.

"What was that?!" screamed Mum, flinging the ham sandwich across the kitchen.

Amy dropped her spoon. She knew it was Õogly in her bedroom. Desperate to beat Colin she whizzed across the kitchen upstairs. Luckily, due to the number of bubbles covering the landing, Colin had only just walked out of the bathroom when he saw her.

"Oh my, was that large crash you, Amy?"

"*Meeeeehhhh,*" replied Amy before darting into her bedroom. She slammed the door fast.

Amy couldn't believe her eyes - the mess! It looked as though Õogly had turned completely silly. In the few short minutes Amy had been downstairs, Õogly had got out of bed and dressed in Amy's grey school uniform. Then she'd tripped over the corner of the bed and collapsed on her homework desk, smashing the whole thing. Wood chips, paper and pens covered the carpet. Amy certainly wasn't worried about Õogly wearing her clothes, in fact she looked really trendy. But she was worried about explaining the broken desk to her parents.

"Everything alright in there Amy?" called Colin, tapping softly on the bedroom door.

For the first time since becoming a goat, Amy panicked.

"Ummm yeah thanks, Colin..." she said, eyes

searching for a way to block the door.

"MEHHHHHHHHH" bleated Õogly loudly behind her.

Amy pounced on Õogly, covering the goat's dribbly mouth with her hand. Õogly squirmed while Amy held on like she was riding a bucking rodeo bull. Twisting and turning, desperate to keep her friend quiet.

"Well, what an impressive goat noise that was, Amy!" said Colin supportively. "In such a short amount of time, you really have developed incredible livestock interpretations of...of...*ahhhhh... ahhhhhhhh...AHCHOO!*"

Being so close to Õogly through the bedroom door was making him sneeze and wheeze like a bumbling elephant with a blocked trunk.

"Where's that *blasted* cat?!" he shouted, turning around. "I stop giving him his bath for two minutes and I'm back to sneezing my head off. Stewart, where are you? You pesky thing!"

Stewart the cat had been hiding in the laundry tub and foolishly took this moment to jump out.

"There you are!"

From inside Amy's room, she heard crashing and yelling as her stepdad chased the cat across the landing and down the stairs.

Amy sighed, rolling off Õogly. "He's gone, you're safe."

Õogly sprung up and started prancing around Amy's room on her back legs like a human.

"What's got into you, Õogly?" giggled Amy.

"Mehhhhhh," the animal replied before balancing a teacup on her head.

111

"You look like the King of England!"

Next, Õogly strutted to the windowsill, still on her hind legs like a lady and started performing ballet. With a front hoof on the windowsill to balance herself, the farm animal bent forward, stretched up and spun on one leg quite beautifully.

"Bravo," said Amy, clapping. But suddenly, her smile started to fade. She couldn't help but feel something was wrong. Very wrong. Amy approached her friend and placed a hand across her forehead.

"Oh no!" she said, snatching her hand away. "Your temperature is back. It's soaring - in the hundreds! You've got more than just the flu."

Without delay, Amy ran to her parent's bedroom. She returned carrying Colin's book on tropical diseases. She slammed it down on her bed making the whole thing wobble, for it was a very large, heavy book. Frantically turning the pages, she skimmed them as she went. She stopped when she reached Sillyitus-Gangu-Fever. She read the description:

Definition: Despite being classified by the Biafran Medical Association as a tropical disease, Sillyitus-Gangu-Fever is most common among livestock in parts of Kent, England. Similar to a severe case of 'the giggles', Sillyitus-Gangu-Fever makes the victim develop silliness and buffoonery. Symptoms, when left untreated, can progress to Super-And-Very-Extreme-Sillyitus-Gangu-Fever.

Cure: Avoid laughter and only commit to dull, sensible, past times. (And a good night's sleep helps).

Amy looked up from reading to find Õogly hanging upside down from the curtain rail.

"Come down from there at once! You have Sillyitus-Gangu-Fever so messing around and laughter will make you worse!"

Goats aren't known for their gymnastic skills so Õogly fell from the curtain rail like a sack of potatoes.

"Get into bed this minute. A good night's sleep is what is needed by all, including me." Amy gave Õogly a good shove in the bum, as she clambered into bed. She looked up at her clock, it was long past her bedtime. "This is serious now. You have to sleep through the night and rest all of tomorrow while I'm at school."

She forced herself to stop talking as hearing the words upset her too much.

"And, I hate to say it, but I also have to behave tomorrow and can't act like a goat." She avoided Õogly's eyes as she spoke. "Just for the day until everything dies down. Mother said every student, teacher and dinner lady will be watching me, waiting for me to mess up and act like a goat."

As she spoke, she heard snoring and looked over to see Õogly fast asleep. Her mouth hung open, tongue flopped to one side. Amy tried to smile but couldn't, she was filled with nerves at what tomorrow would bring.

15
Monday morning breakfast

The following morning Mum was up at the crack of dawn making pancakes. Bowls of golden batter were stacked everywhere in the kitchen - on the table, by the windowsill, and in the fridge. There were even two plates of pancakes on the floor replacing Stewart the cat's food and water bowl. The sweet scent drifted through the house as Mum glided around the kitchen merrily, like Snow White.

"Everything alright, my dear?" asked Colin, peering over his large newspaper.

"She's been right weird all morning," said Sebastián, squeezing maple syrup over his soaring stack of pancakes. Today was the day he was going to be at the top of the pyramid in cheerleading practice so was having double everything.

Colin folded his paper and walked over to Amy's large saucepan of grass soup. He peered into it. "Has this got anything to do with yesterday?" he glanced up at Mum. "Anything to do with Amy being a g - "

"Absolutely fine!" snapped Mum, flashing a smile. She had a lump of pancake batter in her hair. "Everything is a-b-s-o-l-u-t-e-l-y fine."

Then, rather oddly, Mum left the kitchen

without saying anything and placed a plate of fresh pancakes at the bottom of the stairs. She dragged the large electric fan over, plugged it in and angled it so the fan was blowing the pancake scent right up to Amy's bedroom.

"Everything is absolutely fine," she repeated, clapping her hands together.

Colin watched the scene unfold, "Pancakes are Amy's favourite."

"Are they!?" gasped Mum, wiping her sticky hands on the front of her apron. "I did not know that. What a coincidence. I guess she'll have to choose between these buttery-brilliant pancakes and…" she gulped loudly "…grass soup."

Colin rattled inside a drawer and pulled out a spoon. "I think I'll try some of Amy's soup for breakfast. It's not every day she cooks the whole family something nice."

"That's because her food tastes like poo," said Sebastián, taking another pancake.

All at once Amy came trotting down the stairs and into the kitchen. Everyone stopped talking and turned to watch her intently, puzzled at what she may do next.

"Morning Amy!" Colin cheered. "I'm about to try some of your glorious soup, would you like some?"

"I MADE PANCAKES!" blurted Mum, thrusting a plate of them in the girl's face.

"Mehhhhhhh," she bleated, ignoring them both. She trotted over to the rubbish bin and pulled out empty food packages with her teeth. She flung an empty baked bean can across the kitchen. It splatted in Sebastián's maple syrup.

Colin slurped up a spoonful of soup. "What are these tasty brown bits floating in it, Amy? Pepper cloves?"

"They're bits of mud, Colin," said Sebastián, flicking the can back at his sister. "You're eating bits of dirt from the garden. Amy dug them up with her teeth and mixed them with bits of grass she's been weeing on, as she no longer uses a human toilet."

Amy's stepdad held the lukewarm soup in his mouth as he listened to the boy. He reluctantly swallowed. "Well, all the vitamins from the dandelions are sure to give me lots of energy."

Mum clung to the kitchen table, trying not to faint in shock as she watched her daughter scratch her head on the side of the fridge door.

"What have you done with your hair, Amy?" she asked, voice shaking. "It's grown all over your body. And how did you stick on that fake tail?"

"Yes, that tail looks very effective," said Colin with a twinkle in his eye.

"Don't listen to him," said Mum quickly. "If you take it off you can have some pancakes, your favourite. Would you like something sweet on them?"

She flung open what Amy referred to as 'The Forbidden Sugar Cupboard'. Sweeping the cupboard clean Mum made a pile of sugar on the kitchen table. Maple syrup, sprinkles, marshmallows, the expensive chocolate, everything to temp her. "Oh, and there's some blueberries on the top shelf of the fridge. You adore blueberries, don't you Amy?"

Mum stepped over to the fridge, shooing her daughter out of the way. "Shoo shoo, you're just ever so slightly in the way there, Amy. No need to scratch your head so aggressively in public. One might think you have…" she paused. "…fleas."

Meanwhile upstairs, the most wonderful night's sleep was coming to an end and being welcomed by the mouth-watering scent of warm pancakes. Amy squeezed a long stretch right through her body as she woke.

"Ooh, pancakes. My favourite."

Amy stopped mid-stretch as she rolled over to see the time on her alarm clock.

"08.25! I've overslept! Why didn't anyone wake me up? Õogly!? It's time to get up, I'm late for school and I really can't be late, not with everyone watching my every move, they'll use this as a reason to expel me!"

The frantic girl ran to her wardrobe and threw her school tie on around her pyjama top. "Do I look alright, Õogly? I've decided I'm going to express my goat-ness a little bit today - but still thought it good to wear a small bit of uniform…Õogly?"

The sound of clattering pots and pans drifted up from the kitchen. Amy poked her head out of the wardrobe and over to the bed. It was empty.

"Meeehhhhhh," came a loud call from downstairs, far more goat-like than Amy had ever achieved.

"Õogly?"

No answer.

Slowly a wave of dread filled the girl's body. She could hear her mums' muffled shouting in the kitchen. It sounded like she was swatting something with a tea towel. Amy knew where Õogly was.

Thinking fast she darted out of the room to the staircase. She held onto the banister and leaned over the landing to peer into the kitchen. She couldn't quite get a full picture but could hear the heavy clanging of cutlery. Õogly was on the breakfast table.

"Down you get Amy!"

"*Mehhhhhhh,*"

"If you keep licking that jar of marmalade there won't be enough for anyone else!"

Amy collapsed back onto her bottom, feeling dizzy.

"They think Õogly is *me*!"

In the kitchen, Mum refolded the tea towel and placed it neatly in the drawer. She turned and glared at the mess. She had no other reason but to believe she was looking at her daughter dressed as a goat.

"If you're quite done, we'll be leaving for school in two minutes."

Amy had to think of a plan in the next few seconds. If she revealed Õogly's identity to her parents, her family would force Õogly to leave - being so unwell this would kill her! But then, if Amy allowed Õogly to go to school pretending to be *her* she would risk getting expelled. That meant an eternity of home-schooling with Mrs Moopleton, even on Christmas Day!

"There's no question to it," said Amy. "I can't risk exposing Õogly."

At this point Mum called, "Amy, Sebastián, I'm getting in the car!".

"*Oui bien*," replied Õogly, jumping from the kitchen table. She trotted over to the front door and nuzzled Amy's school satchel to fall around her neck.

Amy's mother took a step back in surprise. "Well, Amy it's nice to see you're finally cooperating. Now, where did I leave the car keys?"

Amy had to think fast. Her mind felt like a lit-up flashing pinball machine with a ball darting from one end to the other.

"Think, Amy, think," she said to herself, trying to align her thoughts. Suddenly the idea came to her. It was really very simple. Well, sort of. Quite simply, she had to do absolutely every single minor thing listed below and under no circumstances change from absolutely every single minor thing listed below, even for a second.

> **Number 1**
> *Amy had to get in that car in the next six seconds.*
>
> **Number 2**
> *At school, Amy had to make sure Õogly did not do anything to draw attention to herself and make her more ill. The cure for Sillyitus-Gangu-Fever clearly stated 'dull and sensible pastimes'.*
>
> **Number 3**
> *Amy could not be seen by anyone at any time.*
>
> **Number 4**
> *To achieve Number 1 through to Number 4 Amy had to get moving...NOW!*

At once Amy rushed down the staircase and out the backdoor, seconds before Mum left the house.

"Shotgun!" yelled Sebastián.

"Absolutely, my Little Hero," said Mum. "During this experimental stage it might be best if Amy sits in the back anyway, should any of the members of the Circus Society see."

Mum held open the back door and Õogly clumsily clambered in. Once buckled up, Mum glanced over her shoulder to check that the neighbours hadn't seen.

"Last chance to get changed, Amy. Maybe into something with less hair?"

"*Mehhhhhh.*"

"Lovely," said Mum, pretending everything was very normal. She pushed the car door closed and got into the driving seat. She paused and looked into the rear-view mirror at who she believed was her daughter nibbling her own tail.

Meanwhile, Amy, the real Amy, not the one who everyone had mistaken for a goat, had silently slipped into the boot of the car.

Amy rolled around like loose luggage. Whenever they passed someone they knew, Amy's mum swerved across the road and shouted, 'Everyone hide!" Like it was a new game.

After being fully covered in carpet burns, Amy felt the rumble of the engine die. She could hear the chatter of classmates and teachers all around her. They were at the school gates.

Now the real challenge began.

16
A goat at school

As soon as the car stopped, Õogly leapt out the window and galloped to the school gates.

"Amy, you'll get yourself run over!" shouted Mum thudding the car window from the driver's seat. She still believed she was looking at her own daughter.

Sebastián waited a few moments then unclipped his seat belt and climbed out of the car. He didn't want to be seen with his freak sister. Amy used this time to slide silently out the boot of the car. Then, moving like James Bond, she dashed across the grass (even did a forward roll which wasn't necessary) and slipped into school. All the time she kept a close eye on Õogly. She had to be careful because everyone thought *she* was Õogly and was acting like a goat. If they got caught Amy would be expelled. Plus, Õogly could die from the excitement as she now has the disease Sillyitus-Gangu-Fever.

Loud chatter from children rang down the corridor. Classmates stood by lockers, stuffing bags with books. Every few minutes the corridor went silent as Mrs Moopleton floated by like a hungry shark. Amy hid behind a stinking bin, crouched low, watching Õogly across the hallway. To her surprise, the students took no notice of her goat friend. They were now used to seeing Amy act like a goat. Today they simply thought she was wearing a lot of make-up to look identical to a goat.

Amy heard the yell before she saw what caused it.

"There's a goat in the school! There's a goat in the school! Go get the headmistress… NOW!"

It was Sara, one half of Sarah and Sara the identical twins with almost identical names. She was yelling at the top of her lungs, her arms flapping like a panicked penguin. She pointed straight at Õogly. All the school children looked around in excitement.

"Don't be daft," said Sarah, smacking her sister across the head. "It's freaky Amy-Wamey with the big teeth. She wants to be noticed, don't encourage her." She grabbed her sisters' collar to pull her away.

Wiggling free, Sara continued. "No, I'm telling you, that is a real goat!" she shouted, jumping up and down so everyone saw. "Amy has brought this repulsive animal into our nice clean school." She paused. "Wait, where is *she*?" She swivelled around, scouring the corridor. "The real Amy. She must be hiding round here somewhere?!"

"You sound ridiculous!" shouted Sarah, rolling her eyes.

Amy hid closer to the sticky bin. The twins and Õogly were the most unpredictable people she knew. Anything could happen.

Unaware of who she was dealing with, Õogly skipped towards the bullies. They were standing shoulder to shoulder like a wall, blocking the water fountain. Sarah flicked her hair from her shoulders, ready for a fight.

"What do you think you're doing, Goat-Lover? You haven't asked permission to drink from our water fountain."

Not knowing the water fountain rules, Õogly barged between the sisters to reach the tap. The strength of the animal made Sarah fall back.

"Did she just shove me!?"

The sisters snarled at each other. Finally, they could have the fight they'd been waiting for and even better if it ended in Amy being expelled from school. They shared an evil stare, and everyone knew they were about to do something bad. Well, everyone... except Õogly.

Immediately, all surrounding students slammed shut their lockers, zipped up their bags and formed a semicircle to watch the fight unravel.

"Fight!" screamed Jenny from the crowd. (Jenny was clearly still angry about Amy eating her pencil case). "FIGHT!" she screamed again, making the boy next to her jump.

Sarah cracked her knuckles, ready to strike. The usual punishment for drinking from the twins' water fountain was to be held upside down by your ankles and shaken like a piggy bank. Once your week's lunch money had fallen from your pockets the sisters would drop you on your head and spit on you.

"FIGHT. FIGHT. FIGHT!" chanted the mob of schoolchildren.

"Shake her!" shrieked Jenny.

Clueless to the scene unfolding behind her, Õogly continued to lap up the water with her long tongue.

"Get out of there, Õogly," said Amy under her breath. She'd never felt so useless in her life.

FIGHT. FIGHT. FIGHT!" the children whispered more quietly as Sarah snuck up behind the animal.

But just as Sarah went to grab the goat's tail, the school bell rang for the first lesson.

RINGGGGGGGGGGGG!!!

The sudden noise caused Õogly to leap up in shock. Unaware of the bully standing directly behind her, she kicked out her back legs straight into Sarah's stomach.

"Oof!" the girl gasped, falling to her knees.

Sara looked down at her twin rolling around on the floor clutching her tummy.

"Someone get the nurse!"

But no one was listening. They could smell paint. Thick, grey paint from Mrs Moopleton as she slithered through the corridor, waiting for a child to be late for the first lesson. Children grabbed their books and bags and darted in every direction. Amongst the mayhem, Amy slipped outside to the side of the school building. She knew Õogly's first class was French which was a room on the ground floor with large windows. The plan was to keep watch from outside. Standing on tiptoes, the girl peered in. The walls were lined with French flags and pictures of the Eiffel Tower.

"Miss, Miss," wheezed Sarah, stumbling into the classroom, bent over gasping. "Amy Bloomsy... she kicked me!"

"*Non non, en français!*" (No, no, in French), tutted Madame Papillon, the French teacher. She was busy scribbling today's lesson on the whiteboard.

Rule Number 2 of French class was all students must speak in French. Rule Number 1 was no gum chewing.

"Ummm," stumbled Sarah, biting her lip. "Amy Bloomsy le kick me dans le stomach!"

"Amy!? *Mon favori?*" (My favourite?) Madame

125

Papillon spun round, her thick red hair bobbing around her. She would not hear a bad word said against her most improved student. "*Tu ne dis pas la vérité!*" (You are not telling the truth!)

At that moment, in gallivanted Õogly. She was now having terrible symptoms of Sillyitus-Gangu-Fever. The sudden excitement from the school bell had triggered her to become silly. Very, *very* silly. Amy spotted this instantly as Õogly's pupils burned large like black holes.

"Ahh *Mon Favori!*"(My favourite!) sang Madame Papillon at the sight of her favourite student. She waived a small French flag in joy,"*Ça va?*"(How are you?)

"*Mehhhh!*" bleated Õogly before speaking utter nonsense in French about *abat-jour* (lamp shades) and *petits amis* (boyfriends). Then, without warning, she clambered onto Madame Papillon's desk and started tap dancing. Clomping away, scratching the wooden desk, she sang about which of the boys she'd like to kiss most.

"La la, *Je veux t'embrasser*, Oscar *mon coeur*" (I want to kiss you, Oscar my sweetheart).

Amy watched nervously outside. "She's gone silly from Sillyitus-Gangu-Fever!" She felt her body cringe, "*Eughhh*, everyone's going to think I fancy Oscar Ablebottom! Yuck!"

Despite school rule number 317: Children must not sing and dance, Madame Papillon didn't stop the misbehaving schoolgirl (or who she thought was the misbehaving schoolgirl). She was so impressed by Õogly's advanced use of irregular verbs, she let her continue.

"*Très bon Amy, très romantique*," (Very good, Amy, very romantic) she applauded, falling off her chair from excitement.

With everyone watching, Õogly slipped across the desk towards Oscar Ablebottom. She leant down and gave him an unwelcome lick with her long tongue. The children cheered, except for Oscar who felt the wet saliva on his cheek.

A low murmur broke out as classmates whispered between themselves. They weren't used to this. This thing that made them nervous. This so-called 'fun'.

The whispering grew with excitement and soon everyone was having a brilliant time.

Chloe Bassingthwaighte, a girl forever being painted grey for one thing or another, stood on her chair and broke into song. Mohammed A'bor, the school's best football player, whipped out a frisbee and flung it across the room. Everyone was jumping around screaming, singing and howling. This was the first time any of the students had had fun at school, and it was all due to Õogly. Shrieks of laughter burst through the window to where Amy hid in the bushes. She knew she should be excited but couldn't help but feel sick. A ball of nerves turned in her stomach as the racket grew and grew. It carried across the school while all other classes were silent. Someone was going to hear them. Everyone was dancing, well, everyone except Sarah and Sara. They sat rigid with heavy frowns.

"Miss!" erupted Sarah over the noise. "You still haven't told off Amy for kicking me in the stomach! Miss!"

Madame Papillon was busy doing the conga line.

Sara leant close to her sister and whispered, "I've already told you Sis, it's not Amy. That's a real goat! Amy is smelly, but not *that* smelly."

For once, Sarah listened to her sister. She watched the animal in front of them as it reached around with its long neck to lick its bum. The last time she saw Amy, she certainly didn't have a curly beard. A whiff of sour goat breath floated by.

"I think you're right, Sis," she said gasping from the smell. "That is a real goat!"

Sarah wasn't used to being ignored, especially

when grassing on someone. She shoved her chair back and marched to the large wooden bookcase on the other side of the room. She stared up at it, 4 meters tall, crammed with blue and red French dictionaries. Then, using Jenny's head to help balance, she climbed to the top shelf of the bookcase. She was so high up; the top of her head brushed the ceiling.

"LISTEN TO ME!" she shouted across the classroom.

Everyone stopped, including Õogly. The children stared up to see what profound thing this girl had to say.

"That thing," she spat, pointing at Õogly, "isn't Amy Bloomsy at all, take a closer look, because it's a real-life g-…"

But just before Sarah finished, Mohammed A'bor's frisbee went flying into her stomach, in the exact spot Õogly had kicked her.

"*Oofffffffff!*"

She tumbled down from the bookcase and landed splat on her sister. The whole class once again erupted with laughter. They were now all infected with hysterics.

"Humpty-Dumpty, Humpty-Dumpty!" the children started to chant.

Madame Papillon used her flag, conducting them like an orchestra.

Suddenly, someone banged on the classroom door. It was loud and unfamiliar. Everyone shut up.

In crashed Ms Trudy-Wudy, the P.E teacher.

"*Bonjour!*" cried Madame Papillon flummoxed. She smoothed her wild red hair to look presentable. "*Es-tu perdu?*" (Are you lost?)

Ms Trudy-Wudy dipped her whole hand into a packet of lemon sherbet and licked it. "No, I know exactly where I am." She looked at the sign on the door that read 'Room 116B'. "I'm in Room 116B," she said, tapping the sign slowly with sherbety fingers.

Madame Papillon opened her mouth to speak, but nothing came out. The P.E teacher was in control. She scanned the classroom of children who sat panting like scared puppies. She stopped, having spotted her prey: Õogly, who was still up on the desk, now balancing on her head.

Ms Trudy-Wudy smirked. "Did you know Miss French Lady that there are goat hoof marks across my cross-country trail?" She spoke to Madame but stared at Õogly.

Madame opened her mouth, but the P.E teacher got there first.

"*And* there are goat hoof prints outside on the school green. Is this goat aware it's stomped over the headmistress' private rose garden?" She paused and forced her whole hand into the lemon sherbet. "And those muddy goat hoof prints are down the hallway...past the water fountain...leading here. Straight into this very classroom...Room 116B."

She wiped her sticky hand down the front of her vest leaving a dusty yellow smear.

"So, Madame French Teacher, I have *very* strong evidence to believe that that *thing* is not Amy Bloomsy, but in actual fact, is a real-life GOAT!"

At once Ms Trudy-Wudy blew her whistle, stinging everyone's ears.

"Leave her alone!" screamed Amy.

Ms Trudy-Wudy's head whipped round to see the

girl standing outside, pounding the window.

Sarah and Sara's heads spun from goat to girl, then girl to goat.

"GET THEM!"

17
The chase

"You go that way, we'll go this way!" ordered Sara to her classmates. "Surround them!"

Immediately the children started closing in on Õogly. The fun they'd had moments ago was gone. Now, as if under a spell, they moved towards the animal.

Amy had to think fast. She pushed open the classroom window and yelled. "Õogly, jump out here!"

Quickly the goat slipped and scampered across the wooden desk. Mohammed leapt across to grab Õogly's back leg but narrowly missed. Õogly landed with a thud in the grass next to her. Amy turned and slammed the window shut.

"At least they can't follow us out the...window.... now..." Her speech slowed and stopped like an old train. She didn't believe her eyes. The entire school was bursting out the school doors. Hundreds of children and teachers flooded through, falling over each other.

"They're after us!" shouted Amy, as everyone ran *straight* towards them.

She remembered the reward Mrs Moopleton set for the first person to hand her over if caught acting like a goat - unlimited tickets to Disney World *and* queue-jump *and* unlimited birthday cake, made by Mickey Mouse himself. This is something everyone in the world wants. Imagine the sweet taste of that unlimited birthday cake, topped with sprinkles.

Amy gave Õogly a shove in the bum and immediately they started running. They sprinted away so quickly that they trampled over Mrs Moopleton's private rose garden, again! Amy glanced back at the damage. Instead of noticing the squashed roses, she saw weapons. Teachers had sharpened pencils to catapult at the girl. Others had thick, heavy textbooks to drop on her once they got close enough. Even the school janitor, Miss Plop, was involved, holding a mop and bucket like a sword and shield.

The frantic chase for the goat and girl was in full swing.

"Don't panic!" screamed Amy to Õogly, (though she was really trying to calm herself). "And don't look back!" She said, looking back.

Amy's stomach was doing summersaults. All she could do was run faster and faster. Pant harder and harder. They were panting and running so much, they weren't watching where they were going. And then it was too late. Straight ahead were 49 cheerleaders stacked high and wide on shoulders to form a giant human pyramid. One slip and they'd come crashing down. And where there were cheerleaders, there was Sebastián.

Amy twisted her head in all directions, trying to find him. She had to avoid him or else he'd get the cheerleaders to chase them too. Her eyes frantically searched the limbs stacked high. Arms holding legs, holding heads, holding legs. Row by row she scanned up, getting higher and higher until she was squinting, trying to make out who was at the very top behind the clouds. They were standing proudly, arms on hips, balanced on a single person's head. Suddenly an image of this morning's breakfast flashed in her mind: Sebastián was eating double pancakes. Sebastián said he was going to the top of the pyramid today.

Amy felt her world crumble around her. She looked up and caught a flash of shiny hair. It was Sebastián. This was the moment he'd been training for, his moment to shine.

"Stop!" cried Amy to Õogly over her shoulder.

But she wasn't there. The angry mob of teachers and children were there, but no goat. She turned back around and saw Õogly running in front. She'd overtaken her! And was galloping straight towards the human pyramid.

"Stop! Stop! STOP!"

Like an uncontrollable bowling ball Õogly smashed into the pyramid. Children went flying.

"Ahhhhhhh!"

"Oooooooooh!"

"Eeeeeeeeeh!"

Children fell from the sky like they were tumbling from a giant Jenga. Amy watched Sebastián soar over a large oak tree and fall through its branches, landing with a thud.

His face shot scarlet red as he exploded. "Ahhhh! I hate her! That was my big moment!"

Amy darted past him. Even in anger he didn't look or talk to her.

Straight back into the race, Amy and Õogly had to now run faster than ever. Before Õogly crashed into the cheerleaders they were simply fleeing from teachers, children and a janitor. But now they were fleeing from teachers, children, a janitor, 48 angry cheerleaders *AND* a mean older brother who would do anything to hurt them.

"*Mehhhhhhhh*," cried Õogly.

"Exactly what I'm thinking," said Amy. "Let's keep going!"
And so, on they raced. The afternoon sun was out in full making it an incredibly hot with no shade.

As she ran, Amy wiped her sweaty forehead with the sweaty palm of her hand. Her mouth was dry, longing for a drip of cold water. Õogly was also suffering, but for different reasons. All this excitement was causing her Sillyitus-Gangu-Fever to flare up and make her very silly. She leapt over bushes backwards and landed on her head, then she'd suddenly stop and do the Macarena. Such silliness meant she was very, *very* unwell.

"We need to head back to school," panted Amy, diving to narrowly miss a rock thrown at her head. "There are hiding places and we'll be in the shade. It's our only chance of getting out of this alive!" She spotted an old forgotten sign pointing towards the science block. Amy pictured hiding in the cupboard where the lab coats hung. "This way!"

But Õogly had her own idea. Instead, she ran in

the opposite direction: to the school canteen!

"Where are you going!?"

Õogly went bounding through the kitchen's double doors, terrifying the canteen staff.

"Ahhhhhhh!" came the screams.

CRASHHH came the chaos that followed.

The canteen staff, who had just finished mopping the floor, were enjoying a well-deserved tea break when Õogly charged in. She went sliding across the slippery floor like a goat on an ice rink. Limbs flaring in every direction, she went head first into a stack of clean plates.

"Get that stinkin' animal out my kitchen!" screamed Betty, Head Dinner Lady. She armed herself with a rolling pin and jumped at the animal.

Darting away, Õogly's back hoof pierced a huge bag of self-raising flour. A sandstorm of white powder burst through the kitchen.

"Where ya gone!?" screamed the dinner lady, blinded by the flour. She swung her rolling pin at the shelf holding the water glasses. Glass shattered onto the hard kitchen floor.

"Head for the sports hall!" shouted Amy to Õogly.

Betty froze in the flour mist, recognising the voice. "It's Amy Bloomsy! Should 'ave known anythink goat-related would be her doin'."

Amy coughed and spluttered from the flour sandstorm. She couldn't see the doors anywhere. Then she spotted the bright green exit sign in front of them. "This way!"

Once outside, covered in white flour, they kept running. The list of people chasing them was now even bigger! There were:

- Bitter teachers desperate to get to Disney World
- Classmates and bullies
- One miserable janitor
- 48 angry cheerleaders
- A mean older brother
- Seven sweaty canteen staff
- Head Dinner Lady whose biscuit break was rudely interrupted

Thinking fast, Amy and Õogly clambered down the shadowy staircase leading to the school sports hall. Out of breath, Amy pushed open the doors and dragged her feet to the centre of the basketball court.

"I don't know - " puffed Amy, "how much longer – I need to stop."

It was cold inside the sports hall. Amy felt the heat rising from her body and sweat drying on her face. She bent over, gasping to catch her breath. Inside the gigantic sports hall, she felt very small.

Normally at times like this Õogly would nuzzle her, give her a lick. Instead, she didn't even notice how Amy was trying not to cry. The animal was bouncing a basketball, throwing it at the hoop down the far end.

All at once, Amy heard the muffle of the mob outside. They had found them.

"Quick," shouted Amy, pointing at the pile of blue exercise mats. "We can hide among them."

She ran over to the mats, her trainers squeaked on the polished floor. She lifted half of the plastic mats and then dropped it like a dead weight. Her whole body ached. She already hated moving the heavy mats in gym class, and now she was too tired. She looked back over at Õogly who was ignoring her, shooting hoops.

"Help me, Õogly!"

Amy heard the stomping of feet coming down the staircase.

"Õogly!"

But it was too late. They were at the door, pushing it open.

Amy dived amongst the pile of mats. Õogly spun around to find an empty sports hall. Louder and louder the pounding came. Suddenly alert, the goat scampered around, panicked, eyes searching for somewhere to hide. She looked up and saw a heavy thick rope hanging from the ceiling. She shot up it. At the top, she hung upside down, just like she'd done on Amy's curtain rail. It was a good hiding space…as long as no one looked up.

"I watched them run in here," shouted Sara, marching in. All the teachers, children, and cheerleaders followed the twins into the sports hall.

"Look!" she pointed down to white flour prints.
"Follow the markings, they're hiding." She acted like
an army officer giving commands to dinner ladies.

The mob separated at once. Ms Trudy-Wudy the
PE teacher went straight to her equipment cupboard.
She clambered into the large bin of balls. Like a dog
digging in the dirt, she scampered through the bin
of balls, throwing them over her shoulder to bounce
and roll across the sports hall. Betty, Head Dinner
Lady, followed her but chose the sack of coloured
beanbags.

In plummeted her hand, having a good feel

around. "I know you're in 'ere somewhere! I'm desperate to get my hands on that unlimited birthday cake made by Mickey Mouse!"

Jenny, who had never been so angry in her life, stomped over to the larger gymnastic equipment. She looked under the mini trampolines. She muttered under her breath. "I'm going to be the one to hand you over to the headmistress! I don't even care about the reward anymore!"

Amy remained still and quiet. Chloe Bassingthwaighte sniffed around the mats, getting close to her. She reached out and lifted the corner of a mat covering Amy's toes. She squealed like she'd seen a mouse, *"Eeeeek!"*

Amy buried her foot under a different mat. Maybe she'd got away with it.

But then she realised Chloe hadn't squeaked at the sight of her toes. She'd squeaked at something else. Amy coughed. There was a smell. It was toxic. It was paint.

Suddenly a can of paint was launched across the sports hall. It burst open, splattering thick grey paint across everyone. The empty tin hit and fell against the back wall. In silence, everyone watched it roll around on the floor.

In the doorway, blocking the light, was a woman with a murderous look: Mrs Moopleton.

And stood by her side was Sebastián.

18
Mrs Moopleton has her moment

At once, Mrs Moopleton launched forward, chasing the children. In one hand she clutched an open can of paint. In the other, a wide bristled paintbrush. The paintbrush was plunged then whipped out, wet and dripping. She catapulted herself at the crowd, screaming wildly, waving the brush. The children and teachers stumbled over each other, trying to get away. But she was too fast. She started frantically painting. Every foot, hand, face, and shoe was smeared with cold, wet paint.

"WAHHHHHH!" screamed Jenny with an open mouth quickly filled with paint.

"Calm down will ya!" reasoned Betty, from the catering team. She shouted over the children before slowly turning to see Mrs Moopleton knelt behind her, frantically painting the backs of her legs.

The children slipped and skidded across the silky sports hall floor, racing to the exit. The screams were deafening, made 100 times worst in the echoing hall. Quickly, Mrs Moopleton whipped out a long white roller. She looked like a desperate decorator ready to paint the walls. She dipped the long fluffy sleeve in the grey paint and pounced at the children. Pinning Oscar Ablebottom to the ground, she rolled his entire body. Up his legs, along his arms, over his face. He was left lying on the hard ground covered in a perfectly even coat of paint. Soon all the blues and reds and greens inside the sports hall had disappeared. The green netball court, the coloured beanbags, and the blue mats were engulfed in a dull, heartless grey.

Amy continued to stay very still. She felt herself becoming a bit lightheaded from the paint fumes so started nervously talking to herself to stay awake.

"If I stay here – just - just a little longer, everyone will – I hope - forget about Õogly and w-w-we and we can sneak out."

Suddenly the cries erupted even louder. Amy's ears picked up a squirting sound. She wriggled under the weight of the mats and peered out through a gap. Mrs Moopleton was dragging a very long and very heavy hose pipe across the sports hall. Amy recognised it as the garden hose the school janitor uses to water the headmistress's rose garden. But now, it was being furiously unravelled by the woman to be used for something totally different.

The horrid headmistress found the plastic nozzle at the end. She clicked it into the tap in the corner of the hall. Her upper lip curled. It was ready.

Meanwhile, Ms Trudy-Wudy looked up at her beautiful sports hall dripping in paint. It was now like a dingy, smelly dungeon. She clutched the whistle around her neck, ready to put a stop to the chaos. She took a deep breath in ready to blow when suddenly she was blasted. Grey paint shot out the end of the garden hose, splattering her head to toe. She lifted her large hand and held it up against the blast. Slowly she was pushed back like she was walking against a tidal wave.

Her tummy rippled under the pressure and she fell with a thundering thump.

The whole hall shook. Everyone stared down at
the woman moaning on the floor, covered in paint.
The hose had fired across the hall measuring 25
meters *and* it had been powerful enough to knock the
largest person in Kent to their knees.

Heads slowly turned to Mrs Moopleton who was
standing across the sports hall under the netball

hoop. She blew the end of the pipe like a cowboy. She was dripping in sweat. Immediately everyone raced to the exit, clambering over the coils of the long hose.

But Mrs Moopleton didn't squirt them, instead she rolled her head and shoulders, stretching out the weight of carrying the hose. She was taking her time, almost like she was letting everyone escape.

Then, the sports hall was left in silence.

Drips of paint fell from the ceiling like heavy blobs of rain. Apart from this, there was no noise.

"Where's everyone gone!?" whispered Amy as she peered through a small gap. She started panting nervously, she didn't like the silence. The weight of the mats had become too much. Her face was shoved against the cold floor and it felt like hundreds of sandbags were piled up on top of her. She turned, trying to see Õogly through the gap. She prayed she was still at the top of the climbing rope.

Footsteps started to make their way to where she lay. She couldn't see them, but she heard the slither of the hose being dragged and the tap of high heels. The taps were slow. There'd be one, then a long pause, and another.

"Stop - " came a feeble cry across the sports hall.

Amy heard the shoes stop and swivel.

"Is there something you want to say?" snarled Mrs Moopleton. "Or, perhaps *show*?"

Of course, thought Amy. Sebastián! This was the first time in her life she'd felt happy, even *relieved* to hear her brother's voice. Surely, he would save her?

The boy was free from paint and clean. He hadn't been brushed with a bristle or squirted with a hose. Not a speck. He'd been spared...

144

because he was her spy. For weeks he'd snuck to Mrs Moopleton's office to share secrets about Amy wanting to be a goat. Standing in that room where everything is grey, he'd shown pictures of Õogly and pointed out the Goat Kingdom on a map. When this afternoon's chase started, he'd found Mrs Moopleton. He'd taken her cold hand and led her straight to the sports hall.

Mrs Moopleton squashed an empty paint can like she was squashing a bug. Sebastián jumped awake.

"You want to stay at the top of the pyramid in the cheerleading squad, don't you?"

The boy's eyes shone. She had his full attention.

"And I assume you want to become Captain?" She turned away, knowing he was watching her like a dog eyeing up a bone. "It's very simple really. Just… find…her." She overpronounced her words, spitting at the boy. He stared back, not quite understanding.

"NOW!" She erupted. "You have three seconds to bring that girl to me." She started unravelling her hose. "AND THE CLOCKS ALREADY TICKING! THREE…"

At once Sebastián leapt into action, running around. He had no idea where his sister would hide. He never listened or looked at the girl, how was he going to *think* like her!? He leapt and cartwheeled over empty paint cans towards the equipment cupboard. He searched inside soggy sacks, throwing cricket bats and balls across the room.

Mrs Moopleton got the hose ready. "TWO!"

He stopped suddenly, picturing the random behaviour of his sibling and her goat friend. He had to think differently. He had to think of fun. His cheeks flushed red, he'd worked it out. He jumped over coils of the hose and slid to the centre of the hall. Slowly, he looked up.

"ONE!"

There, at the top of the rope was Õogly. She was hanging upside down, sleeping like a bat. She was oblivious to the paint mess below her.

"Stop! Don't hurt her!" Amy exploded from the pile of crash mats. She was out of breath and her hair was stuck with sweat on her face and neck.

The woman's top lip curled again. She knew this was game over. Amy looked so tired; Mrs Moopleton could blow her over with a single breath.

"You stupid -" She started when Amy's mother suddenly burst into the sports hall.

"EXPELLED!" she shouted, marching across the polished floor, arms waving in a fury. She was dressed in a sparkly leotard, and upon her head was her tall headpiece made of long ostrich feathers and plastic beads. She stomped towards them, cursing under her breath. Only when she approached, could Amy hear what she was saying.

"EXPELLED! Expelled they tell me! Well, I hope you're proud of yourself. I get a phone call at circus training, balancing on my head and I hear the word EXPELLED," she took a gulp of air and then continued. "EXPELLED! And all for a...GOAT!?"

Amy felt a sharp stab in her stomach. She'd been expelled!? She glared at Mrs Moopleton. The resting smirk on the woman's face proved it was true. She'd been expelled from school.

"I–I–um," stuttered Amy, trying to think straight. Õogly snored loudly from the ceiling. Amy looked up, remembering where she was. "Mum, her name's Õogly and we have to help her." She pointed up at her only friend. "She's got Sillyitus-Gangu-Fever – it's deadly and - Mrs Moopleton will paint her – then kill her and - "

Mum stood flummoxed, watching words spill out of her daughter's mouth.

"Such nonsense!" she bellowed, throwing her hands in the air, knocking a string of beads from her headdress. "I don't want to hear it. It's the big circus opening tomorrow and I can't afford to be stressed! AND RIGHT NOW - I'M STRESSED!"

And with that, she grabbed her daughter by the arm and pulled her towards the exit.

"I'm sorry for this mess Mrs Moopleton, your Highness," she called over her shoulder with a curtsy. "Oh, and also for my outfit. Had I been expecting my daughter to get expelled, I would have worn something far more formal."

"Let go of me!" squealed Amy. She scratched at her mother's tight grip, "I can't leave Õogly!"

Mrs Moopleton watched the mother and daughter in disgust. "The home-schooling will begin tomorrow morning. First I will see to this...'goat'."

"No!" shouted Amy, frantically trying to squirm

free. She turned to Sebastián, her eyes desperately searching his. She tried to see something in his eyes that showed he cared about her, even the smallest bit. She pleaded, "Sebastián, *please* help. Õogly will die if I leave her!"

This whole time Sebastián hadn't uttered a word. He was staring down at his own feet. He felt ashamed. Why had he helped Mrs Moopleton? And for so long. He wanted his sister expelled but he never wanted the goat to be hurt.

"Sebastián, *please!*" Amy cried.

He watched his sister use the last of her energy, trying to squirm free. She'd never once given up. Suddenly their eyes locked across the hall. He was looking at her and she was looking back behind tears. This was the first time in their lives they'd looked at each other. He felt something jump in his stomach. He ran his hand through his shiny smooth hair, took a deep breath in and announced. "I will help the goat and save - ".

"Get out," hissed Mrs Moopleton, interrupting his big speech.

He looked aghast.

"I will help - " he tried again.

"Get. Out."

He stopped, embarrassed. That's twice now he was interrupted.

Amy's mother glared at her son, frustrated at his time wasting. "Oh, be quiet, the pair of you. Sebastián, go and get in the car."

"But I..."

"Be quiet, Sebastián. No one cares anymore. Go and get in the car."

And with that, he hung his head low and scurried out of the sports hall.

Mum grinned awkwardly at the headmistress, desperate for her approval. "Lovely. Soooo we'll see you bright and early tomorrow morning. 7am for the first lesson of Extra-Complicated-Mathematics?"

"Better make it 8am," replied the teacher, clicking the plastic nozzle of the hose in place. "I have to finish something first." She smirked coldly up towards Õogly.

Mum followed the woman's gaze and paused. "Urm...but you are just joking about this whole 'destroying' the goat thing? You're having a laugh, aren't you?! It's a harmless goat!" She laughed nervously to herself.

"When have I ever 'had a laugh?'" replied Mrs Moopleton.

"Oh," gulped Amy's Mum. "I see."

"No!" screamed Amy, now really panicking. "Leave her alone! She's my only friend!"

Hearing her best friend upset, Õogly suddenly awoke and slid down the rope, ready to help. She landed with a thud in a can of paint. She was unaware of how much danger she was now in.

"What are you doing, Õogly?" shouted Amy.

"Climb back to the top!"

"Quiet now, Amy," soothed Mum as she pulled her daughter away.

Then, the sports hall door was closed and they were gone.

19
The large cardboard box

The following morning Amy sat sulking in a very large cardboard box. In the dark she'd scrunched her body tight into a small ball, hiding from the world while the sun shone through the sitting room windows.

"Could you pass me one of my new dusters, Amy?" asked Colin, softly.

Amy didn't reply despite being surrounded by dusters and cloths. Her stepdad had placed a large order of cleaning products to be delivered to the house. Now Õogly had gone, Colin was cleaning everything. He'd learnt the true cause of his sneezes (he also owed Stewart the long-suffer cat an apology).

He tapped lightly on the side of the box, "Amy, my dear?"

No response.

He sighed and started wiping the box itself. "You know I was home-schooled, there's no shame in it. In fact, because of home-schooling I know every Latin word for every type of bacteria. Why there's *Flexithrix* and *Herpetosiphon-geysericola*". He paused and peeked down through the slit of the box lid, smiling. "Oh, and there's *Lactobacillus-coryniformis-coryniformis*, if you want to get really fancy".

"*Colin*," whined Amy. "Please stop."

"Ah, so you are alive! You have not suffocated among my new dusters?"

"No."

Colin felt sad that she didn't reply with her usual cheery goat cry. Quickly he moved on. "Excellent! So, while you're sitting with my new dusters, you lucky girl, you can tell me what happened at school yesterday? Was it those blasted twin bullies again? If I ever get my hands on them!"

Amy didn't reply. She scrunched herself tighter, burying her head. She wanted to hide in this box like it was a cave.

At this point Mum stomped down the stairs into the sitting room shouting at the top of her voice, ruining the peace. Her arms were full of bulging black bin liners. "I've collected all the hay and straw and half-chewed items of clothing to be thrown away. *And* I've put Amy's bed sheets in the wash!" She marched over to the large cardboard box where Amy hid and shook it manically, "AMY, WON'T THAT BE NICE, TO HAVE CLEAN BED SHEETS?"

Amy toppled over as her world was rocked like an earthquake.

After the mess she'd caused at school, Mum had banned her from ever being a goat again. The straw had been removed from her bedroom, the grass soup was flushed away, and Amy was back to walking and washing like a human. The change had left the house, and Amy feeling empty.

"What's wrong with the girl?" asked Mum, glaring at Colin, but not wanting an answer. "Did she lose her hearing when she turned back into a human?" She looked down at the large box in the middle of the room. "Well you better get your hearing back soon, Amy. Mrs Moopleton phoned to say she's on her way for your first lesson." She lowered her voice to speak to Colin. 'And the g-o-a-t business has been taken care of."

Upon hearing this Amy scrunched back into her protective ball. A single tear fell from her eye. It ran sadly down her cheek and landed on the cardboard floor leaving a dark, wet circle.

"My dear," hushed Colin. "Perhaps we could put off the first lesson for a day or two? Amy lost her best friend and self-identity, all in one afternoon."

"And have the girl do what? Sit around playing with slime for 17 hours?"

"Well, I thought you could take her to circus training, as it's the big opening tonight."

Amy's mother swung round, arms flapping like a wild goose, "Absolutely not! Today is my last chance to perfect balancing on my head while riding on a camel! And because of her..." she thrust her hand and pointed at the box "...we're miles behind schedule. The whole circus is blaming me. I had to leave yesterday to pick-up my expelled daughter!" She glared at Colin who had his back to her, busy wiping down the bin bags she'd just brought down. "Why don't you get it!" She rummaged around the pile of coats looking for her large feather headdress. "The show starts at 4pm, don't be late. I've reserved you and the kids front row seats." She found her headpiece and left in one of her moods, slamming the front door so hard it made the whole house shake. The living room was left in silence, other than Amy quietly crying.

After a long wait, and the sound of her mother's car fading Amy said. "I don't even know what happened to Õogly," she sniffed. "Mum forced me to abandon her with Mrs Moopleton."

Colin slowly walked over to his stepdaughter, head hanging low. He could picture her pulling away, not listening to a word she was saying. He sat on the floor cross-legged and leaned against the box.

"I know, Amy," he said with a sigh, causing the box to bend under his weight. He paused, Amy could sense he was about to say something. "I- I- know I'm not your birth Dad but..." he nervously stopped. "But I-I've always tried to be the best dad I can be when it comes to you and Sebastián. But I've truly failed you with this one." He sighed and rubbed his forehead. "I should have been there to stop it."

They sat back-to-back, separated by the cardboard wall of the box. Amy felt his chest rise and fall as he cried quietly. Her throat tightened and she wanted to reach out and hold his hand. She never wanted Colin to feel responsible.

"I will do all I can to find that goat friend of yours," he continued, blowing his nose into a yellow duster. "Even if it means disguising myself as the school cleaner and searching every grimy, dirty hiding place at your school."

"*Ex*-school!" corrected Amy, allowing herself a little laugh.

"Ahh yes! Good riddance to them!" He threw the snotty duster across the room in protest.

Suddenly, just when Colin thought he was making progress, Sebastián exploded in through the front door, dripping in sweat.

Colin jumped up, "Sebastián! What are you doing back? You left for Extra-Extra-Early-Cheerleading training just a short while ago." He glanced down at his wristwatch. "Your mother tells me you're at the top of the human pyramid today thanks to your little bribe with Mrs Moopleton?"

"Where's Amy?" he puffed, ignoring Colin, looking round the sitting room.

"What's wrong? Calm down!" he followed after the boy, placing his dirty rubber glove on his shoulder to calm him.

Sebastián sprung back, "Eww gross, Colin!" But then he spotted the large cardboard box.

"Is that Amy!?" he asked.

"Well, your sister is *in* the box, yes. She hasn't left her goat life for one of a cardboard box."

Sebastián grinned, "Don't speak so soon!" He ran over to the box, pulling open the lid to call down to his sister. "Amy! You have to come to school at once, something amazing has happened!"

"Go away!" she snapped, reaching up and

shutting the cardboard lid quickly. She plummeted back into darkness.

"Amy, you have to believe me!" He jumped around, shaking the box. "Something incredible has happened at school. You need to see it!"

Amy was getting pushed around from his jumping. She was feeling irritated. "It's not *my* school anymore, thanks to *you*." She hissed, holding the cardboard walls to balance herself. "Besides, since when did you talk to me? I thought I wasn't good enough to be spoken to... Oh, unless you're plotting to kill my best friend."

Colin made an awkward face at Sebastián. She had him there.

Sebastián exhaled deeply and stepped away from the box, giving his sister space. Amy felt the distance. Like most people, Sebastián struggled to say sorry. He wanted to say it, he had it on the tip of his tongue, but he couldn't get his mouth to form the word. He bit his lip and glanced over at Colin, half expecting him to say it on his behalf. But really, he knew what he had to do.

"I'm sorry Amy!" he blurted loudly, scrunching up his face, eyes slammed shut.

Amy said nothing. She deliberately let the words hang in the air.

He relaxed his face and opened one of his eyes. Colin looked back at him with a twinkle in his eye. He nodded his head towards the box.

Sebastián shuffled forward. "I'm sorry for everything," he continued, suddenly speaking more seriously. "For taking Sarah and Sara to the goat pen, for telling Mrs Moopleton you were in the sports hall."

He paused and touched the box like he was reaching out to his sister. "For not letting you be yourself as a goat."

"For killing Õogly!" snapped Amy.

Sebastián's head shot up, surprised at his sister's words. He abruptly opened the cardboard box lid and shouted down to his sister. "That's what I'm trying to tell you! Õogly is alive! She's still at school!"

The sunlight stung the back of Amy's eyes. She raised her hand to shield her face.

"I don't understand," she said, squinting. "I thought Mrs Moopleton killed her?"

"Not yet she hasn't! You becoming a goat has started some sort of rebellion at school - it's fabulous!" Sebastián started bouncing around the living room excited. "Kids are doing whatever they want - actually, it's complete mayhem - some kids are being dogs, others are birds and sat in the trees." He paused for a breath, "Oh, Oscar Ablebottom, who you fancy, has become a refrigerator! He's sat in the middle of the canteen humming to himself like a fridge. Hmmmmmmm, he goes." He took a large gulp of air and continued, "Hmmmmmmmmm."

Amy frowned, confused, "A refrigerator!?" Then realised what her brother said. "I don't fancy him!"

"You're missing the point," Sebastián continued, running back to the box. "All our classmates are happy and laughing and being themselves. It's all because of *you*."

Amy didn't hear the last bit, all she could think about was her best friend. "And Õogly is there?" she asked, looking up at her brother for the first time.

"She's somewhere amongst the mayhem," he replied with a big shrug. "Everyone thinks Mrs Moopleton has her locked in a cage in her grey office, ready to be covered in cement."

"Cement!?" questioned Amy.

"Oh...you didn't hear?" Sebastián's face fell like he was dreading being asked. "She said paint isn't strong enough."

"Strong enough for what!?"

Sebastián sighed and looked away from his sister as he spoke. "Mrs Moopleton wants to cover Õogly in grey cement and leave it to harden so that she becomes a statue. She'll then be placed in the private rose garden..." he looked up. "The one you two trampled...as a reminder to follow the school rules."

Amy covered her ears, not wanting to hear anymore.

"Õogly will slowly turn into a statue, but first have to watch all the children being miserable and - "

"STOP!" shouted Amy, "Stop talking!"

Colin scratched his head having listened to Sebastián speak. "What kind of weird school does your mother send you to?"

"But there's still time!" continued Sebastian, ignoring Colin. "She needs you, Amy."

Amy shook her head, still hiding in the box. "*Me*? All I do is make things worse. It's because of *me* that Õogly's in this mess." She paused, then spoke as if it was the last time she was ever going to speak. "I can't do anything."

Sebastián couldn't believe her words. As a goat, his little sister was so confident and sure of herself. Now she sounded completely broken. Slowly,

Sebastián leant down into the box, wrapped his arms under her shoulders and heaved her up. She felt so small. He wanted to shake some sense into her but instead pulled her in for a hug.

He let the girl tremble and felt her tears sink into his shoulder. Then, he looked deep into her eyes, "Amy," he said, stopping to make sure she was looking at him. "Goats don't spend their days hiding in boxes. Goats listen to their brothers. Goats change the world."

Amy wiped her soggy nose and a long string of snot was smeared along her sleeve. Sebastián silently gagged in his sister's face, remembering how smelly she really was.

Amy couldn't help but smile.

"You're wrong," she said.

Sebastián's mouth opened, ready to plead again.

"Goats definitely *don't* listen to their brothers!"

Amy leapt out of the box and cried, "I'm a goat and I'm coming, Õogly! *Mehhhhhhhhh!*"

20
The smirking door

Immediately, Amy, Colin and Sebastián scrambled into the car.

"Shotgun!" shouted Amy and Sebastián together, lunging for the front seat. Sebastián shoved Amy out of the way to reach the car door first.

"Back to old ways then!" said Amy jokingly.

Colin slid carefully behind the steering wheel. He twiddled the hanging mirror and sprayed his square driving classes with some polish.

Amy and Sebastián watched the man, biting their lips impatiently.

Colin reached under his chair and pulled out a mini handheld hoover.

"CAN WE GET GOING NOW PLEASE!" burst Amy over his shoulder from the back seat.

Colin jumped, dropping the hoover in his lap. "Ahh, yes of course."

Carefully, he pulled out the drive and finally they were off! Amy and Sebastián jumped around excited, whereas Colin drove 15 miles below the speed limit.

"Come on, Colin," whined Sebastián. "People are *walking* faster than us."

Amy glanced out the window to see them overtaken by a man with one leg pushing a buggy.

Colin reduced his speed further. "Everyone needs to just breathe and calm down. Who knows what we're going to find when we get to your school?"

Amy folded her arms feeling frustrated when, out of nowhere, her ears picked up a sound. Quickly she rolled down the car window and it was louder. It was the sound of laughter. She could see the school down the road and the closer they got, the louder the laughter became.

Suddenly Amy felt the tug of her seatbelt around her chest as the car jerked forward. It felt like the car had jumped off the road from an explosion.

Colin grabbed the gear stick to gain control. "Must be ice on the roads. That's the problem with black ice, you don't see it until you're on it."

Amy looked up at the scorching sun. "But Colin, it's boiling."

"I think that's the worst of it over," he continued, not listening.

Sebastián turned around to Amy and said smugly: "What you just felt was Chloe Bassingthwaighte."

Amy stared back, waiting for him to continue. When he didn't, she asked. "What? She's decided to become something slippery on roads?"

"No, stupid," replied Sebastián rolling his eyes. "She's become a magician! I expect one of her spells went wrong and there was a bit of an explosion." He pointed out the window. "Look, see."

Amy glanced up to see Chloe standing by the side of the road stirring a smoking cauldron. Her cheeks and nose were brown with soot.

"Drive faster, Colin!" Amy shouted in excitement, kicking the seat in front of her.

Ever so carefully Colin pulled up outside the school gates. "Now before we open the doors," he said taking his keys out of the ignition, "let's all wear these germ-protecting suits I brought and…" But before he'd finished, Amy and Sebastián had leapt out, slamming the doors behind them. "I'll wait here in the car then!" he called after them, reaching back down for his hoover.

"Let's go to Mrs Moopleton's office straight away!" Amy said to her brother. "If Õogly's locked in there it'll be easy-peasy to get her."

But suddenly Amy stopped. She looked at the scene before her and felt silly for what she'd just said. There were children everywhere. And they weren't acting like humans. There was so much excitement in the air, just like in Madame Papillon's French class when everyone started having fun.

"Duck!" yelled Sebastián suddenly, breaking Amy's thought.

Amy swung around to see Mohammed from her class dressed like a duck. He was flying straight at her.

"Oh yes a duck, so I see!" she squealed with delight, before being whacked in the head by a flipper on the boy's foot.

"I meant duck your head!" said Sebastián, pulling his sister up.

Amy stumbled up onto her feet. "Oh my, I really didn't see him coming - "

"Move!" shouted Sebastián again. He quickly pushed his sister out of the way before a girl pretending to be a train came storming past.

"Chooo chooo," she chugged, as she raced past, turning her arms round and round like the wheels of a train. She smashed straight into a small boy pretending to be a daffodil.

"Flowers shouldn't grow on train tracks!" she shouted down at him.

Amy stood motionless, watching the chaos. She felt like she'd been dropped in a zoo where all the cages had accidentally been left open and both animals and zookeepers were running around in a panic. Children were acting like dogs, birds, unicorns, slimy snakes and hammerhead sharks. Those that weren't acting like animals were acting like witches, rusty teapots, steam engines, magicians, pretty flowers, and even kitchen utensils. Amy swore she saw three sisters dressed as a fork, spoon and knife.

One might think the students had become a bit silly. But it was wrong to think that way. The children were simply being themselves. And children are a bit odd when they are *finally* allowed to be themselves. Free to become whatever object or animal that springs from their imagination. As Amy watched she realised this is what she'd always wanted. It was fantastic. She felt the burning sun on the back of her neck so slipped under a tree for some shade.

"Oooooh, your hair's tickling me," giggled the tree. Amy jumped up to see Jenny, the goat-hating girl in her form group. She had transformed herself into a tree. All her skin was painted a mossy green colour and she'd stuffed her hair, ears and nose with green leaves.

"Oh, sorry," stumbled Amy stepping back, embarrassed to be giving Jenny *more* of a reason to hate her. After all, it was just yesterday when Jenny wanted to hand her over to Mrs Moopleton.

"Don't you worry. Would you like a lemon?" Jenny slowly pulled a lemon from her left sock and handed it to Amy, "I'm a lemon tree."

Puzzled and a bit weirded out, Amy grabbed the lemon and ran. As she ran around the side of the school building, she tripped over a lazy boy lying very still in the grass.

"I'm a stone!" he shouted after her. "I can never be bothered to stand up."

Amy opened her mouth, ready to tell him what a stupid idea it is to want to be a stone when she realised it was no sillier than being a goat.

"*Mehhhhh,*" she bleated like a goat.

Suddenly Sebastián called from across the school grounds. "Amy, over here!"

Amy swung round to see her brother make his way towards her. Like an obstacle course, he cartwheeled between two teapots, narrowly missing Jenny the lemon tree then backflipped over the lazy stone boy.

"What?" he said to Amy once perched beside her. He wasn't even out of breath. Amy stared back at him in shock. Finally impressed by his cheerleading skills, but she didn't want to tell him that.

"There are the school doors," he continued, pointing across Mrs Moopleton's private rose garden.

There was just one final obstacle.

The obstacle was called Kane, the current Cheerleading Captain.

Kane decided who was in or out. After Amy ruined the giant human pyramid, Kane kicked Sebastián off the team.

"It's payback time," hissed Sebastián through gritted teeth.

Kane had chosen to become a flamenco dancer and a very good one at that. He was wearing a frilly red flamenco dress and stomping around biting a single red rose.

165

The performance would have been very good had he not been blocking the school entrance.

"*Olé!*" he sang, clapping his hands and jumping in the air.

"Shall I go chew his dress?" suggested Amy. "That'll get him out the way."

Sebastián waited a moment, watching the boy, then said slowly. "No, leave it to me."

Immediately, Sebastián grabbed the lemon Amy was still holding and threw it at the dancing boy. The lemon bounced off a tree (or was it Jenny?) and landed square in Kane's face. Sharp acidic lemon juice ran into his eyes.

"My eyes!" squealed Kane, wiping them frantically. Panicked, he spun around in circles and then tripped on his long dress, falling flat.

"Great shot!" cheered Amy, fist-punching the air.

"Wooohoooo," whistled Sebastián, joining in with laughter. Crouched low, hiding from the chaos, the pair shared a smile. Amy felt something warm in her stomach. The brother and sister hadn't smiled together since…well, ever. The moment felt quite magical. However, it didn't last long as they needed to move fast while the school entrance was clear.

"Come on!" said Sebastián, grabbing her wrist.

They exploded into the school. Amy ran on all fours as a goat, headfirst into the double doors. Sebastián backflipped down the corridor, causing all the children's artwork pinned to the walls to flap around. They darted upstairs, coming to a stop outside the door to Mrs Moopleton's office. You felt the grey before you saw it. Children sent to the headmistress's office often came back sobbing, telling tales of this door and how it sucked out their happiness just standing near it.

"Õogly!" shouted Amy, shaking the handle back and forth. She twisted and turned it then rammed her body against the windowless door. "Are you in there?" she called through the keyhole, squinting to see in.

There was no reply.

"Shhhhhh," hushed Sebastián, tapping Amy on the shoulder.

Frustrated, she banged the door with her fist, then kicked it. The door simply stood there, smirking at her, refusing to open. Amy looked down at the chipped grey paint from where she'd kicked.

"Shhhhhhh!" went Sebastián again, louder this time. "Be quiet!"

Amy spun round to her brother. "What's wrong with - " Quickly he placed his hand over her mouth, cutting her off.

He turned and stared down the deathly quiet hallways.

"It's a trap," he whispered. "And we've cartwheeled straight into it."

21
Chaos in the corridors

"Õogly!" shouted Amy, banging on the door.

Sebastián grasped Amy's hand, stopping her.

"Shhh, Amy," he whispered. "I think we're being watched."

The pair had been so focused on saving Õogly, they hadn't noticed the eerie feeling in the school. It was silent as if the school was empty. But at the same time, it felt very much like there were people everywhere. Watching them.

Amy's head snapped up at the sound of something down the hallway. The lights were off at the end so she couldn't make out what she was looking at. But something in the dark was moving. Someone was screaming.

"CHARGE!"

Suddenly Sara and Sarah were charging straight at her. The identical twins with almost identical names exploded down the corridor like Roman chariot racers. The row of school lockers bounced around as the floor shook. One fell over, the door bursting open and books spilling out. Charging with the twins were the school's first-year students, about 50 of them. The first years were the youngest kids at school and did everything the twins said. They were too young to know better so blindly followed orders. Plus, they fought dirty. They fought like terrible toddlers with biting, scratching and eye gouging. Just what the twins liked.

"Get ready!" shouted Sebastián over the racket. He watched the stampede come at him. His knees were bent, arms out, ready for the battle.

Amy's mouth hung open. "What!?" she screamed in terror. "We're not seriously taking on the first years!? They eye gouge!"

But before Amy had finished, everyone had leapt into action.

"CHARGE!" yelled Sarah.

Every first year with their sticky, unwashed hands leapt on Sebastián.

A small boy acting like a chihuahua dog dashed straight for his ankles. Two girls wearing wizard hats started bonking him on the head with their wands.

"Meeeeeow," snarled a scrawny girl with sharp fingernails. Teachers were forever telling this girl to cut them but now she was a tiger, circling Sebastián, ready to pounce.

"Get out the way!" cried Amy to her brother.

But Amy had nothing to worry about. Sebastián was thinking fast, using his cheerleading skills to fight back.

First, he high-kicked the chihuahua dog boy smack in the face, smashing his glasses. Then, he side-lunged to the left to miss the tiger girl. Then, he did a back flip, knocking off a rat-like child who'd been crawling up his back, trying to get to his eyes for a good gouge. When the rat child was on the floor squirming to get free, Sebastián grabbed him by the ankles, spun him round in circles and flung him along the hallway like he was throwing a heavy shot put in athletics class.

"What are you doing!?" screamed Sarah to her weakened army. She punched a locker in anger, leaving a big dent. "Get off the floor you useless bunch of FREAKS and get Amy the goat!"

She pointed straight at Amy who was standing alone in the open at the far end of the corridor. All eyes landed on her. She'd become prey. Her heart was thumping out of her chest as the first years crept slowly towards her.

"T-t-there, there," she hushed the kids like she was hushing an angry dog backing her into a corner. A girl with pigtails slithered on her belly like a python. A snotty-nosed boy swung from a ceiling light like a chimpanzee.

There was a terrible snarling noise. Amy felt a shudder up her spine. She spun round to see eight boys knelt behind her, dribbling.

"*Hooooowwwwwlll,*" they cried like a pack of wolves

170

ready to rip her apart.

She took another step back and smacked into a metal locker. The locker was right up behind her now. There was nowhere else to go. Her eyes darted from the python girl to the wolf boys who were baring their sharp, sugary teeth. Her heart leapt; she couldn't control her breathing. Amy certainly didn't want to hurt anyone, she just wanted them to move out the way so she could get to Mrs Moopleton's office and save Õogly.

"Amy!" called Sebastián across the hallway. He was holding a first-year upside down by her ankle. "You're a goat! So *be* a goat!"

Amy listened to him. In the real world, a pack of wolves would tear a little goat apart. But right now, the only way out was to act like the greatest goat of all time.

"*Mehhhhhhhhhhhh!*" she cried, shaking the school. It was by far her best goat cry yet!

Sarah and Sara pulled an awkward face. They knew they were in trouble now.

Thinking fast Amy clambered down to all fours and raced down the hallway, head first. She charged towards the first years the way Õogly had charged into the human pyramid. As she galloped, she remembered that day at Godstone Farm. The fear in everyone's eyes but twinkling excitement in hers. The bullies hadn't beaten her then and they wouldn't beat her now.

"Come get me!" shouted Amy with her dirty teeth filled with old grass.

The young wolf boys seemed to suddenly snap awake. They looked around at the mess and darted in the opposite direction. Amy and her brother chased after them. They were close enough to smell sugar and fear. The first years ran towards the twins who'd been cowering under the water fountain.

"Stop!" cried Sarah. "Retreat!" She pulled her sister, Sara in front of her like a shield.

"Let go of me, Sis!" screamed Sara back to Sarah, also pulling Sarah in front of her like a shield.

"You're the one who said she was smelly!"

"You're the one who *told* me to say she was smelly. I've always loved the smell of farm animals."

"That's a lie! Amy, she's lying!" pleaded Sarah or Sara, squirming behind one another.

At this point, it didn't matter who was talking as Amy was charging like a bull and not about to stop when suddenly –

HONK HONK!

Came a noise from outside.

HONK HONK!

"Amy, Sebastián, have you finished?" called Colin, honking the car horn. "It's nearly four o'clock, we need to get going to your mother's circus show. It's the big opening!"

Amy stopped; the moment was lost.

"What are you doing!?" yelled Sebastián at his sister. "Finish them off! This is the moment you've been waiting for."

Amy glared back at the twins. For months they had picked on her. Spat at her. Made her want to stay home and cry. Shamed her for having big teeth. Made her hate herself - like it was bad to be different. Wrong to be a goat. She felt her anger build but at the same time didn't want to hurt the pair. She didn't want to be like them.

172

"Didn't you two hear me from the car!?" Colin stumbled into the corridor. He was wearing a white face mask to protect himself from the germs. "I've been honking for ages," he continued, sounding muffled from the mask. He suddenly stopped and looked around. Battered children were lying on the floor, rolling around and weeping. They had grazed knees and missing teeth. Lockers were knocked over, books spilt everywhere. It looked like a war zone. "I say, what's happened here? Some kind of war play you're practising?"

"*Colin*", whined Amy, embarrassed like he was the first parent to arrive at a birthday party to pick her up.

Colin pointed at the dog boy Sebastián had sat on. "That boy's bleeding from his ear, is he meant to be bleeding from his ear?"

"Yes, yes, he's fine," said Sebastián, pushing Colin out of sight. "You can wait in the car."

"There's no point arguing, kids. Your mother's performance starts in six minutes. She'll be wondering where we are."

"But we haven't found Õogly," moaned Amy. "The twins have her, I'm sure of it." She glared over at the two girls who were hugging each other, faces wet from tears.

"Oh, I haven't told you," said Colin, stepping over a child. "I have reason to believe that your goat friend isn't here at all. In the car, I received a very odd phone call from your mother."

"What!?" said Amy, head snapping up. "What did she say? Where's Õogly?"

"I couldn't make it out, a bad signal from where she is inside the circus tent. But we'll see Mum in a minute. We can pop back after the show if you want to continue playing with your friends." He smiled at the twins and ruffled Sarah's hair.

Sarah and Sara were white as paper, trembling in terror at what Amy and Sebastián might do next.

"Oh, he-he-hello Mr," stuttered Sarah. "I'm Sarah, and this is Sara, my sister, we're twins."

Slowly Colin removed his hand from the girl's head. The twinkle in his eye died. He recognised those names. He'd spent evening after evening comforting his stepdaughter from these bullies. Washing her cuts and holding her with hugs, telling her not to listen to their mean words, trying to help her anxiety. He wasn't about to let them leave without telling them exactly what he thought.

He stared down at the bullies, making them feel very small.

"You two are *cruel* little girls."

The bullies jumped at his sudden change of tone.

"Cruel, horrid bullies," he continued, his hands shaking in anger. "There's nothing smart about what you do and believe me when you grow up, you'll look back and be ashamed."

Sarah opened her mouth to speak but quickly closed it, thinking twice.

"W-w-we're sorry -", stuttered Sara, not meeting Colin's eye.

"Oh, you will be. But you'll only be sorry for yourselves."

Amy couldn't believe her ears! The only thing worse than being told off by your parents is being told off by somebody *else's* parents.

Colin turned his back to the bullies, leaving them

looking very foolish.

"Come along, Amy and Sebastián, it's important we show your mother our support."

And with that, Amy trotted after her stepdad, leaving the bullies behind.

22
Opening night

"Where's Õogly!?" yelled Amy, jumping out of the car.

Sebastián and Colin clambered out, their shoes squelched in the thick mud.

"Eww gross," whined Sebastián, shaking his foot. "Wherever Amy goes, mud follows."

Not listening to her brother, Amy quickly galloped across the car park towards the giant, red circus tent. Ferris wheel music was playing loudly from the speakers. There was a long, winding queue stretching across the field. She forced her way through it, desperate to get inside.

"Excuse me," she said, pushing through a family with two sticky children. "Don't mind me." She sucked in her tummy and slipped through the crowd. Once inside the tent, it was just as manic as the queue. Clowns were squabbling, people were yelling, and children were crying.

"*Wahhhhhhhh,*" cried one child who shoved into Amy. She had a stick of pink candy floss stuck in her hair. Her parents shouted down at the girl. "Don't pull it! You're making it worse!"

Amy's eyes darted through the maze of people. The smell of warm, salty popcorn filled her nose. Occasionally there was a strong waft of animal poo.

"How am I going to find Mum in this mess!?" She said to herself, trying to see through the crowd. Just as she started to put a plan together, there came a loud announcement over the speakers.

"Good evening lords and ladies, boys and girls. Three minutes until tonight's performance begins. That's three minutes, yes three minutes. Please take your seats."

"Three minutes!" shouted Amy in panic. Then, across the tent by the popcorn stand she spotted her mother. It looked like she was having a very serious talk with Norman.

Amy slipped through the crowd. As she reached her Mum, she noticed how tense the air felt. Norman and her were having one of those serious adult conversations - the kind where children aren't allowed to interrupt. But Amy was far too excited about the thought of seeing Õogly so blurted. "Mum! Where's Õogly? Colin said something about you knowing?"

Mum ignored her daughter's questions. She didn't even look at her. "The camel couldn't have just disappeared, Norman," she huffed, waving her arms frantically.

Norman sighed heavily, "I've told you, my dear. I put Yasmin the camel in her pen last night and when I got there this morning to feed her a plate of scrambled eggs, she'd disappeared."

"That's not good enough Norman! My performance needs a camel! Whose hump am I going to perch on while balancing upside down on my head?"

Norman stared at the woman, unsure of how to answer such an odd question.

"Well!?"

Amy's head had been swivelling back and forth, following whoever was speaking. Now there was a pause, she took this chance to interrupt, "Mum! Where's Õogly?"

"Not now Amy!" she snapped back. "Can't you see we're in the middle of a circus catastrophe? And why are you back on your hands and knees acting like a goat!"

Mum was dressed ready for the show, wearing her glittery leotard and feather headpiece. As she shouted at Amy, a row of plastic beads fell from her hat. Amy found it very difficult to take her mother seriously when she wore this outfit.

"But, Mum - " she continued, this time jumping up and down like an excited puppy.

"Please Amy, just wait."

"But I - "

"Not now, Amy."

"But Mum you're not even listening to me."

"SHUT UP, AMY!"

Amy jumped back, shutting up instantly. She didn't dare say another word.

Suddenly another announcement came. "Two minutes until tonight's performance, boys and girls. The show is about to begin."

"For heaven's sake!" huffed Mum throwing her arms up in defeat. "I'll have to figure it out myself. Like always!" She turned on her heels and marched off to the rehearsal tent to warm up.

"Best of luck!" called Norman, cheerily.

Once Mum was out of sight Amy turned to Norman. The last time she'd seen him, he'd brought a giant camel into the kitchen.

"Why does she act like that?" she asked him softly, feeling very small.

"Act like what?" replied Norman, taken aback. "She's a very busy woman, Amy. You have to understand that, everyone can feel stressed." He brought out a small paper flip chart and started ticking things off a long list.

"But she's *always* stressed. She never does anything to help me." Amy paused, "I hate her."

Norman chuckled at the girl, "You don't mean that, she's your mother." Norman glanced round the tent.

"Are all the clowns in from outside?" he queried.

Being laughed at made Amy feel worse. She felt like Norman wasn't taking her seriously because she was a child.

"I do hate her!" she continued, resisting the urge to stamp her foot. "It's because of her that Õogly's lost. Or worse... dead!" Amy felt a large lump in her throat at the thought of her best friend being gone. She tried to hold in the tears but it was too painful. "She's dead, isn't she?" she cried. "Mum's not telling me because she's selfish and only cares about her stupid circus show!"

"Selfish? Your mother!?" laughed Norman, spotting a clown and making a note. "She's the least selfish person I know! Why she missed the last circus rehearsal to go and save that goat friend of yours I'll never understand."

"She did what?"

His eyes glanced up from the clipboard and he looked at her for the first time since starting the conversation. "That goat friend of yours. Oooogle, Ugglee- "

"Õogly," corrected Amy, with a big sniff.

"Bingo! Oooglee. Well, when your mother brought her to me, I instantly ran for my book of Tropical Diseases and diagnosed her with Sillyitus-Gangu- Fever. One of the worst cases I've ever seen. She was rolling around on the ground laughing like a possessed witch. She's all better now and sleeping in the elephant pen." He went back to his list, unaware what he'd just said was everything Amy had been waiting to hear.

"WHAT! She's alive!?" shouted Amy, bursting

with energy. Norman jumped and dropped his pencil in the mud. "You mean you didn't know?"

Amy shook her head. "Not at all. What happened?"

"You'll have to ask your mother for the details. All I know is she went marching into that strict school of yours with a no-nonsense face on and demanded Ugleop-"

"Õogly," corrected Amy, again.

"Yeah, that's the one," he said, bending down to pick up his muddy pencil. "She demanded that Ougl-the goat, be handed over at once. Rumour has it she also got that headmistress of yours sacked. Reported her painting habit to the police! All the circus society has been gossiping about it. But like I said," his tone suddenly darkened, "to save that goat she missed the last and *most* important circus practice. She's very unpopular with everyone. If things go wrong tonight, it will all be her fault."

Amy fell back against a stack of plastic juggling clubs. Her legs felt like jelly as the bottled-up anxiety left her. She couldn't believe what she was hearing. Would *her* mother save Õogly? She thought she hated goats.

Norman continued. "Your goat friend's over in the elephant pen resting, she's all better now."

Amy jumped up. "Where's the elephant pen?"

Norman pointed with his muddy pencil towards two clowns juggling outside. "Just past Jakub and Diego – ahh, I knew I had two clowns missing from my list – just past them - you can't miss it."

Hearing this, Amy galloped past the clowns

to where Norman had pointed. He was right, you couldn't miss the elephant pen. It was an enormous wooden pen the size of a house. Piles of hay lay scattered around it and across one side were strong metal bars. Amy stopped momentarily and nibbled a piece of hay. She suddenly felt quite nervous. She couldn't help but imagine short-tempered elephants guarding her friend.

"Õogly?" she called softly, fully aware she'd spoken too quietly for anyone to hear.

She edged closer to the pen and touched it. Immediately one of the elephants made a deafening trumpet noise. It started stomping its giant feet, making the cage shake.

"Shh, shh," hushed Norman bumbling over. He looked down at Amy. "They can smell you."

"Everyone says that," she replied.

Norman led the girl round to the far side of the pen. They were standing in front of the metal bars and inside Amy saw two gigantic African elephants with long, sharp tusks. One was standing tall and wide, swinging its head and heavy ears. The other, smaller one was dozing in the corner. Its heavy, grey belly rose and fell as it dreamt.

"I can't see Õogly," said Amy, bravely poking her head through the bars.

"Well you'll have to go in and find her," replied Norman.

Amy's head snapped back. Suddenly she wondered if her mother's lifelong friend was a bit odd.

"I can't go in there, they'll eat me alive!"

Ignoring the girl, Norman flipped open a plastic

cover and typed in a six-digit code. With a loud clunk, the metal bars of the cage started to slowly rise. When they were about half a metre above the ground, they stopped.

"Go on," he encouraged, nodding his head towards the gap. "You won't have any problems; elephants love to be friends with goats. Doesn't everyone know that?" he joked with a wink.

For some reason, Amy felt like she could trust Norman. She bent down and carefully crawled under the bars, into the pen. The larger elephant that was swinging its trunk stayed where it was. The one sleeping in the corner snapped awake as Amy stepped on the crunchy straw. It didn't stand and charge at Amy, as she'd imagined in her head. Instead, with its long, wrinkled trunk it pointed to its belly.

Amy's mouth fell open. "You've eaten her?"

The elephant rolled its eyes and pointed again. Amy's eyes followed the trunk and to her shock, she saw a third, baby elephant curled up. Under the calf's large floppy ear, she spotted a chunky, muddy hoof.

"Õogly!" She cried, dashing over.

Õogly shot her head up at once. Upon seeing Amy, she clambered onto her scrawny, wobbly legs and leapt into her arms.

"I'm so happy you're alive!" gushed Amy, kissing her friend all over. "And out of everyone, it was my *mother* who saved you! Can you believe it!?"

"*Mehhhhh*," bleated Õogly, nuzzling the girl.

Norman wiggled his way into the elephant pen himself. When doing so he looked like a large worm squirming on its belly.

"Sorry to break up the moment," he puffed, shaking off bits of hay, "but your mother would be *awfully* disappointed to not see you in the audience. She's been practising for months."

"I feel terrible," confessed Amy, looking up at Norman. "I need to speak to her first. Tell her I'm sorry – wish her luck." She turned back to face Õogly for advice. "What do I do?"

"*Va lui dire*," (Go tell her) replied Õogly. She lifted her front hoof and pointed at the smaller rehearsal tent where Amy's mum was warming up.

Amy nodded in agreement. "Okay, so before the show starts -" She paused, suddenly realising how quiet it was. She glanced over and saw the busy queue of guests had disappeared. "Where's everyone gone?"

"They're inside," said Norman. "The show's begun..."

23
The ask

Amy licked Õogly goodbye and galloped to the rehearsal tent. She was ready to push open the tent curtain door but then her body froze from anxiety. She was about to have the conversation with her mum she wished she'd never have to have. Her heart was beating violently. She swallowed hard. The noise of a clown being booed off stage played in the distance.

Like ripping off a plaster, quickly she pushed the curtain to the side and jumped in. The heavy material fell behind her, there was no turning back.

The noise and mess inside the rehearsal tent hit Amy like a pie in the face. Golnessa from the local bakery was waking up her vocals singing a scratchy, "*Ooooo, eeeee, ooooo!*" Mr Bucket the postman was lunging from side to side, stretching his skinny thighs. And a donkey in the corner was standing patiently while a clown wrapped a big yellow bow around its long head. Amy had to be careful not to trip over the props scattered across the grass. There were yellow juggling balls and red clown noses everywhere.

Being a small village, Amy recognized everyone. And, unfortunately, they recognised her. Some unlucky people had been at Godstone Farm when the messy goat stampede broke out. Others were classmates' parents who'd heard tales of Amy eating their child's textbook. No one looked happy to see her.

"What's she going to do this time?" Mr Bucket audibly said to himself, as he stopped stretching to apply mascara to his stubby eyelashes. "Stand in the corner *baaing*?"

Standing in the corner 'baaing' is the behaviour of a sheep, not a goat, thought Amy, but this wasn't the time to correct him. Not when all eyes were on her, waiting for her to do something 'strange' or 'weird' or, heaven forbid…goat-like. Instead, she smiled politely like the well-behaved schoolgirl she never was and walked on. She needed to find her mum.

She searched the tent with her eyes. They landed on something wobbly in the corner.

"Mum!" shouted Amy loudly across the tent.

Mum's eyes shot open. She had been meditating while balancing on her head in a headstand. Upside down she watched her daughter trot towards her as a goat.

"Can it wait?" She groaned, still balancing. "I'm in 'the zone.'"

"No, it really can't. I… urm…" Amy stopped. She glanced over her shoulder and noticed some people were suddenly very close to her. They were pretending to warm up and stretch but were actually listening in with their big ears.

"Why are you so concerned with everyone else, Amy?" snapped Mum, watching her daughter. "It's not all about you."

Amy glared back, taken aback. "I never said it was all about me. *They're* listening in!" She pointed at Mr Bucket, who quickly started rolling his bald head around, warming up his neck.

"Oh, you love the drama, Amy! Always have."

Amy paused, suddenly feeling teary. This wasn't meant to be an argument. There was so much nice stuff she wanted to say. Firstly, to say sorry, then to thank her for saving Öogly's life.

She swallowed hard, ignoring the lump in her throat. "I wanted... urm. Well - here's the thing..."

Mum stared at her stuttering daughter. "I'm disappearing back into the zone." She closed her eyes, falling back into a trance, "*hummmmmm.*"

Amy took a deep breath and shook her body to try and relax. Why was she finding this so difficult? After all, this wasn't Mrs Moopleton, it was just her mother.

"I love you, Mum!" she blurted then slammed her eyes shut and screwed up her face awkwardly.

Mum didn't reply.

With shut eyes, and a stiff body Amy continued to blurt and blurt like she'd been holding everything in for so long. "And... I know you saved Öogly even though you'd never admit it because you hate goats - so I just – you know, well wanted to say thank you because – you know, I know you hate me because I'm a goat and you'd rather I spent my time going to some weird lesson like Monkey-Drawing Lessons so I'm really grateful and...urm sorry. Did I already say I was sorry?"

Mum's eyes shot open. Speaking so honestly wasn't normal in their family. She pushed her body forward and lowered herself to the ground. Kneeling upright she rearranged the wedgie from her glittery bikini bottom. "I love you too, Amy."

Amy winced in shock, she hadn't expected that.

187

She'd expected to be wafted away like a bad smell. She looked up at her mum whose face was the colour of a purple turnip from being upside down so long.

"I send you to a colourful selection of exciting and somewhat 'unusual' activities, so you can learn who *you* are," continued Mum. "You won't get that sat in front of the TV all day."

Amy frowned confused. "But…you're always trying to control me."

"Control you!? Heavens no! The complete opposite. I send you to trumpet playing and pogo stick classes to set you free. To open your mind, to try something different! I want you to be who you want to be, Amy. You only work that out by trying lots of different things."

Mr Bucket wiped a single happy tear from his eye as he listened to the kind words.

Amy glanced down. Now was her chance to ask *the* question. Before she could let her brain talk her out of it she blurted. "Can I be a goat!?"

Mum jumped like she'd received an electric shock. This was the question she'd hoped never to be asked. She peered over her shoulder around the large tent. Amy didn't know if she was checking to see if anyone had heard, or if she simply couldn't bear to look at her disgraceful daughter.

"Ooooh this just got interesting!" whispered Mr Bucket, rubbing his hands together.

Mum lowered her voice before replying. "Ummm, if it means acting like a goat *occasionally* - outside of school - preferably at the weekend in a field where it doesn't affect anyone, then go ahead."

She stood up, brushing the straw from her knees, looking past Amy's head.

"That's not what I meant," shouted Amy up at her. "And you know it. You said you want me to be me."

Mum sighed. "Wouldn't you rather be a lawyer? Or a high-earning accountant? Or the world's BEST stamp collector?"

Amy said nothing. She wanted Mum to hear her own words.

And suddenly, she did.

Mum bent down to Amy's level, suddenly serious. She took her daughters hand in hers protectively. She was in the wrong, she now realised this. Her daughter was happy and that's the most important thing in the world.

"I'm sorry Amy, I've been foolish," she spoke softly. "I've been sending you to all these different classes so you can learn who you are, but now I see that you already know." She looked deep into Amy's eyes. "It was me who didn't see that. If you are happy being a goat, then of course, I want you to be a goat."

Amy's head snapped up. "Really!?"

"Yes, really."

"And you don't hate goats?"

"I certainly don't hate goats," her mother defended. "I perform wonderfully with goats, very flexible animals. I simply do not *appreciate* them in my nice, clean kitchen CHEWING THE EXPENSIVE TEA TOWELS."

"Goats don't chew tea towels," giggled Amy, trying her luck with a joke.

"I know one that does!" teased Mum, ruffling

her daughter's hair. "And another thing, I would never let Mrs Moopleton hurt your goat friend. I thought the whole painting thing was a big joke - until I saw the horror in her eyes and clocked what Colin had said about her being a failed artist!"

All at once, a trapeze artist with bulging arms stormed into the rehearsal tent. Norman bumbled behind, trying to calm the man down.

"It went *fine*, no one even noticed," assured Norman.

"I dropp'd the wee fella! He slipped from me grasp!" replied the trapeze artist, waving an empty, ripped leotard that had belonged to his trapeze partner. "How can ya look at me and say no one bleedin' noticed!? He landed naked in the front row didnae?!"

Norman opened his mouth to respond but no words came out. Instead, he stood there, looking like a fish gasping for air. "YOU'RE RIGHT!" exploded Norman. "The show's a CIRCUS CATASTROPHE!" He collapsed dramatically onto a bale of hay. He whipped out a tiny pink fan and fanned his sweaty head.

Amy's mother marched straight over to him. "What on earth has got into you, Norman!?"

"Haven't you seen?" he moaned, thrusting his hand to point at the main circus tent. "Every act has been a disaster. D-I-S-A-S-T-E-R"

"Surely not?"

"Look around you!"

Mum turned around to look at her fellow performers. She had been so busy with Amy; she'd failed to notice everyone crying in panic.

"Who's hidden my left stilt!? I can't go on stage with only one stilt. The laws of gravity won't allow it!"

"My unicycle has a flat wheel!"

"THE ELEPHANTS ARE ESCAPING!"

"Everyone's lost their marbles!" said Mum, gobsmacked. "What can we do?"

At this, Norman's ears pricked up. He stopped fanning himself and heaved himself up. He walked over to Mum and placed his sweaty arm around her, pulling her close to his belly. "Well, I'm glad you asked. You see I really feel it's all down to you now…"

Mum stared at her friend, confused.

He continued. "You know…to save the show."

"I beg your pardon?" cried Mum, batting his arm away. "In case you've forgotten, Norman. I am camel-less."

"Couldn't you use one of the other animals?" pleaded Norman as an escaped elephant charged past. "An elephant perhaps?"

"I wish it were that simple," she sighed. "The dance took months for that camel and me to learn. I purposefully chose *the* most complicated dance I could think of. None of the other animals know it."

As the pair shared ideas back and forth, Amy stood listening. She had watched her mother practice the dance every day and night for months. Not out of

191

choice, but because her mum practised in the kitchen at breakfast, lunch and dinner. Every time Amy opened the fridge to get to her grass soup, she'd have to squeeze past her mother's wiggling hips. Thinking about the routine, Amy remembered it started with dancing the Macarena, then doing the splits and juggling with sharp knives, followed by the headstand...

Suddenly a plan came whizzing to her.

"I can do it!" she cried, causing Norman and Mum to stop squabbling and look at her. "I know the whole routine! I've watched you practice it over and over. You even practice the arm movements when driving the car!"

"That doesn't sound very safe," protested Norman.

"I know it off by heart," continued Amy, ignoring Norman.

Mum looked down at her daughter and smiled politely. "That's nice, Amy, but I don't see how that helps." She turned back to Norman and spoke formally. "So, you see Norman, it's just not going to be possible."

Amy forced herself between the pair, pushing Norman's belly aside. "You're not listening to me!" she screamed up at them.

The pair stopped talking and looked down at the girl, baffled.

"We can replace the camel with a goat."

"What a brilliant idea!" cheered Norman clapping his hands. "I'll go and fetch Oogleewooglee, your goat friend, so you can explain the routine quickly."

Amy pulled at her own hair in frustration. "That's not what I mean! *I* will be the goat."

"Oh, what's got into the girl?" he asked looking at Mum. "Some kind of goat humour I don't understand?"

Amy's mother bent down to her daughter. For the first time in their lives, she understood Amy. "You would do that for me?" she asked softly.

Well, only if you'd let me..."

She looked down at the ground nervously waiting for her mother to change her mind. Amy being in the show would mean the whole village knows about Amy being a goat. Was her mum ready for this?

"*Ohhhhhh,* I get it!" shouted Norman. He shook Amy's shoulders in excitement. "*You* will be the goat to replace the camel – genius!"

"There's just one problem I have with this," said Mum.

"Oh," whispered Amy. Her excitement faded as she waited for her mum to tell her no.

"We should be on stage...NOW!"

24
The show must go on

"Lords and ladies, with great excitement I welcome to the stage - our final act this evening - it's Mrs Bloomsy and Yasmin the camel - oh no – wait – *really*? But she's not a goat– ohhh, sounds a bit odd if you ask me - " the sound of rustling papers "…it's Amy The Goat!"

Amy's mum launched herself through the black curtain and onto the stage. She threw her arms high and roly-poly-ed to the centre of the ring like an unstoppablehedgehog.Onceinthemiddle,shegrinned an unnaturally wide smile. A bright spotlight shone on her sparkly blue outfit. Everything else was left in dark.

Amy hid, nervously peeking out behind the back curtain. The circus ring was vast. It suddenly felt much larger now *she* was the one on it. She was surrounded by an audience of a thousand people. Far and high row after row parents and children were stacked on benches. So high the children at the very back could reach up and touch the top of the canvas tent. If Amy stepped out onto the circus ring, there'd be nowhere to hide.

"*Psssssst,*" hissed Amy's mother out the side of her mouth. "That was our cue." She spoke the words without moving her lips.

Unfortunately for Mum, her daughter had developed stage fright. Seeing Mum practice in the kitchen was *very* different to this. In the kitchen, Stewart the cat might stay awake long enough to catch a few twists and turns. But here at the circus, there were thousands of eyes. All watching her in the dark and mumbling under their breath about how rubbish she was going to be.

"What have I got myself into?" Amy whined to herself. She was so nervous she was shaking. As she clutched the black curtain her hands shivered in panic. Images of the dance raced around her head uncontrollably. An arm, twist, jump...then what? A leap, and turn...what next? One image that kept returning was Mum saving Õogly. Amy hadn't been there to see it, but she could picture it clearly. Mum storming in the office. Mrs Moopleton dropping a wet paintbrush in shock. Mum had saved Õogly; now it was Amy's time to save Mum.

Slowly, the nervous girl bent down to her hands and knee. She was now a goat, and her mum fully accepted her as one. Trying not to think, she trotted through the heavy curtain and onto the stage. She kept her head down until she reached the centre. The audience was deathly quiet, not even the sound of rustling popcorn. Amy sensed the audience was irritated, waiting for this last act to end so they could go home.

"Smile," muttered her mother through gritted teeth. She had been patiently holding her position (balanced on one leg, arms up, BIG grin) while waiting for Amy to join.

Amy looked up but couldn't see the audience. Everything was too bright. Like staring at a car's headlights, every time she blinked, she was met by bluey purple splodges. She glanced up at her mum standing beside her, expecting a comforting smile. But she was in character, grinning out at the audience. Her lips were moving ever so slightly. Like she was counting, waiting for something when suddenly -

The lights dimmed, the music pumped, and they were off! Without warning her mother sprang into action, dancing the Macarena. Her arms moved from head to hips and before Amy knew it, Mum had jumped to face the other direction to do it again.

"Heyyyy Macarena!" she sang, in her finest Spanish accent.

Panicked, Amy's mind went blank. On all fours her body felt glued to the ground as the heavy, thumping music shook her bones.

"Heyyy Macarena!" cried Mum again, this time jumping to face Amy. "What are you doing!?" she exclaimed. "You're meant to be facing the other way!"

The words simply washed over Amy. Everything was happening too fast. She realised she was staring out at the audience like a zombie. In the front row on a rickety bench was a girl Amy's age. She sat with her arms folded, yawning widely. She reminded Amy of herself when she was dragged along all those months back.

"Amy!" came a cry from the opposite side of the stage. "Amy, over here!"

Amy snapped awake and turned to where the call came from. She squinted, trying to see through the light. She could make out the outline of people waving frantically. She held her hand against the light's glare. Colin, Sebastián and Õogly were sat in the front row waving at her. Sebastián was dancing.

"It's like this!" he shouted, moving his hands to his shoulders and then hips.

Colin watched Sebastián then leapt up to join in. "Heyyyy Macarena!" he cried, muddling the steps.

"You know it Amy!" shouted Sebastián. "Be the goat we know you are!"

Amy turned to the audience, suddenly awake. He's right, she thought, I can do this.

All at once Amy leapt into action. She pushed out her arms, flipped them over, touched her head then hips and shook her bum. She smiled and sang along with Mum, doing the same steps.

"Heyyy Macarena!" they cheered together.

The audience however was not impressed. After all, they had expected to see Yasmin the camel dance the Macarena. Not a nervous girl acting like a goat.

"Get off the stage!"

"Boooooo! Boring!"

But Amy didn't care, she looked across at Mum who was glowing with excitement, proud of her goat daughter. Amy was no longer doing this for the audience, this was for Mum. The more Amy danced, the less nervous she became. She trotted (while dancing) across the ring for the next part of their performance.

"Here I go!" cried Mum, before completing a string of perfect cartwheels and landing in the splits. Amy followed by juggling sharp butcher knives *while* balancing on a large rubber ball. As the music got faster and the routine odder, the audience took notice. Those who had been asleep woke up. And the rude ones who'd booed were now cheering.

"Yeahhhh!"

"Wooooo!"

Adults were clapping and crying! Children were stomping and laughing! It was an eruption of excitement and it was all down to Amy the Goat and her mum.

Before they knew it, the finale was upon them. Amy looked over at Mum who was biting her lip. Now it was her turn to look nervous. With all the months of practice, Mum had not once perfected the art of standing on her head while balancing on the hump of a camel. This was Amy's fault. And everyone said that. Acting like a goat and being expelled from school, meant Mum didn't have time to get it right. So, if the next three minutes went wrong, Amy was to blame.

Suddenly the lights dimmed, and the music stopped.

It was time.

Mum and Amy locked eyes from opposite sides of the stage. Sweat dripped from Mum's chin but Amy felt confident as a goat. The audience saw what was about to happen and started to clap. They clapped together as one, starting slow, getting faster and faster. As if they were watching live bear baiting. They were desperate to be entertained.

Mum prepared for the run-up. Amy got in position.

Then... they went for it.

With four wide lunges, Mum jumped on the mini trampoline. For such a small spring, she bounced incredibly high, flying across the circus ring. In the air, her feather headpiece went flying (as planned) and she started to turn her body like an Olympic diver. She had to land on Amy's back, while balancing on her head.

Meanwhile, on all fours being a goat, Amy

frantically scurried around in circles, eyes darting up to her mother, trying to guess where she would land. It was all down to her now; she had to catch Mum on the spine of her back without any mistakes. Feeling confident of her place Amy stopped when suddenly – Mum went soaring past her! *"Mehhhh!"* bleated Amy like a panicked goat.

Like a cannonball, Mum continued to fall from the sky. She soared past Amy two... three... TEN meters further than should have been! If Amy didn't move now, her mother would land splat on the ground. This had to work, she was desperate for it to work. Piercing images filled Amy's head. She pictured her mum missing, hurting herself, people booing, Õogly leaving the family. Amy galloped faster than she'd ever galloped as a goat before. But something was wrong. Her vision was muddled and started to blur around the edges. She looked up, but couldn't see because of the piercing lights. She kept galloping; tripping over juggling balls and skipping ropes. She was running blind. Unsure of where she was heading, she quickly stopped and looked up. She searched above her, hoping for the best. But it was no good; her mother was too far away and still falling.

"Go left!" cried Colin. "No, further left!"

"No, you need to go right!" ordered Sebastián. His arms were flapping, and Amy could hear the terror in his voice.

Amy could neither hear where their cries came from nor see where they pointed. She panicked, not knowing what to do. Not only was the act about to be ruined, but her Mum could be seriously injured.

The audience was holding their breath. Eyes glued open, not wanting to see but also desperate to watch. Suddenly they all gasped at once –

Õogly clambered over the ringside and leapt into action. Colin lunged forward to grab her back hooves, but she was too fast. She galloped into the ring. She looked up at the falling woman, trying to guess where she would land.

Seeing what was about to happen, Amy gave the order.

"Over there, Õogly,!" she shouted, pointing to the left.

Õogly did as told, running to the left.

"Now go back a bit!" Amy continued.

The audience continued to stare, mouths hanging open.

Õogly stepped back half an inch with not a second to spare. Like a delicate dove, Amy's mum fell from the sky and settled perfectly on her head, onto the back of Õogly the goat.

The audience erupted with applause!

Never had such a perfect head landing happened on the back of a goat! The whole tent shook as people jumped to their feet to cheer and scream. They threw roses and handfuls of money at the stage. Some parents pushed their way to the ringside, thrusting forward their new born babies, asking that they be kissed by the stars of the circus.

"Amy the GOAT – Greatest of All Time!" they chanted. "Amy the GOAT – Greatest of All Time!"

Sebastián and Colin clambered over the ringside and onto the stage.

"You did it!" cheered Sebastián, high-fiving his sister.

Before Amy knew it, she was whisked up onto her mother's shoulders and paraded around the ring. There were flashes from photographers and kids holding out autograph books, waving their pens. Amy felt like she was in a dream, removed from her body and watching everything from afar.

"Well done, Amy!" shouted Mum up at her. "You are an amazing goat! I'm so proud of you and Õogly! The pair of you will be joining the Circus Society at once!"

"Õogly?" questioned Amy. "Wait, where is she?"

Amy looked down, trying to see through the crowd of people around her.

"Achooooooo," came a familiar sneeze behind her.

Amy twisted around and saw Colin. To her surprise he was bent down on his knees, wrapped in a passionate hug with Õogly.

"I'm so proud of you, Amy," he said, planting kisses on Õogly's floppy ears.

Amy jumped down from her mother's shoulders. "Colin!" she called over, waving. "I'm over here!"

Colin slowly opened his eyes as if waking from a peaceful dream. He saw Amy and jumped.

"*Mehhhh,*" cried Õogly, licking Colin's leg.

"Oh – I apologise," stumbled Colin, wiping his mouth with the back of his hand. "Easy mistake to make, now there's *two* goats in the family."

Upon hearing this, Amy realised she'd never felt happier.

- The End -

Hello Goat Fan!

Did you enjoy this story?

Why not buy a copy for a friend,
or goat who has a birthday coming up?

This is Louiseee with three e's
first novel and every little helps.

Please, thank you &
MEEEEEHHHHHHH.

DID YOU KNOW THAT BY
BUYING THIS BOOK YOU'VE

SAVED A GOAT?

We're proud to partner with the
UK's ONLY Goat Charity

5% from EVERY sale of 'AMY THE GOAT:
Greatest of all Time' goes to this wonderful
charity who spend their days rescuing
abandoned, abused and neglected goats!

Visit their website for more information on
their amazing cause and to find out how you
can further donate:

www.buttercups.org.uk

Charity No. 1099627

...and, because goats are polite creatures,
I musn't forget my thank you's:

To Jane
Remember that first version and I paid you about £50 to read and edit the WHOLE thing. £50 was a lot of money back then.

To Philly, Spalding & HB
For never questioning, nor doubting that the book wouldn't get made and for reading everything I ever wrote. Worm Digging is still my strongest story yet.

To Ptarmigan & Skye
The first children to read this book and my biggest fans. Please have 'Amy the G.O.A.T' themed birthday parties until you're 18 and encourage your friends to do the same.

To The Parents
For giving me every opportunity in the world. For sending me to a colourful selection of exciting and somewhat unusual activities so I can learn who I am.

To The Sisters
For always pushing and supporting me. For never saying no when I've asked for help, for your guidance and time. Thank you for always being there.

To The Brother

'For his love of mass spectrometry, which I borrowed for the smart goat'. For not being like Sebastián.For also encouraging your children to have 'Amy the G.O.A.T' themed birthday parties until they're 18.

To Noodles the Cat

For keeping me company on sunny Saturday mornings, encouraging me to write, when all I wanted to do was play outside with you.

...and most importantly, **to Hamm**

If it weren't for you, this book would still be sat, unread, on my very heavy laptop. You not only pushed me to publish but made everything possible. You knew before I did, that this would make me truly happy.

Oh, and of course, to you **Dear Reader**

For taking a chance on a brand new author and introducing the world I created, to your children. I hope you have had as much fun reading the adventures of Amy and Õogly, as I did writing them.

Made in the USA
Monee, IL
30 May 2023

34964903R00132